7/1/89

ROCKY ROMANCE

There wasn't a light on in the girl's cabin when Rebecca and Josh reached the clearing. "I guess Kathy's in bed already," Rebecca whispered. "I'll see you tomorrow."

"Wait a minute," said Josh, putting a firm hand on her arm. "Will you look at this moon?" He pointed to the wide open sky above them.

Rebecca looked up. The moon was so pale and pure and beautiful that it took her breath away. They stood together for a long moment, then Josh turned toward her. Rebecca could feel his eyes on her face, and a chill ran down her spine. When she turned and met his gaze, she knew he was going to kiss her.

Bantam Sweet Dreams Romances
Ask your bookseller for the books you have missed

Rocky Romance

Sharon Dennis Wyeth

BANTAM BOOKS

TORONTO • NEW YORK • LONDON • SYDNEY • AUCKLAND

RL 6, IL age 11 and up

ROCKY ROMANCE
A Bantam Book / October 1988

ISBN 0-553-26948-8

Published simultaneously in the United States and Canada

Printed and bound in Great Britain by
Cox & Wyman Ltd, Reading

Rocky Romance

Chapter One

Josh Kramer, the first baseman for the Hudson Falls team, stepped up to the plate. It was the bottom of the ninth inning and there was one man on base. Hudson Falls High was trailing Phillipstown by one run in a game that would determine which team took first place in the division. The crowd was breathless with tense expectation. Josh glanced up into the stands, caught the eye of a pretty, petite girl, and smiled broadly. Then as the fans leaned forward in their bleacher seats, Josh tapped the dust from his cleats with the bat and casually adjusted his helmet. He took his stance, narrowing his light gray eyes at the pitcher in a challenging stare.

The first pitch was thrown. Josh swung hard, the bat hitting the ball with a sharp crack. The ball flew up, up—and out of the park! The bleachers exploded in sound and motion. The air swirled in a blizzard of confetti. The home team rushed out on the field as Josh approached home plate. He whipped off his helmet as the girl, looking beautiful and provocative even in a plain denim skirt and cotton sweater, managed to fight her way clear of the crowd. Her long brown hair, silky smooth and straight despite the humidity, swirled alluringly around her.

Josh's teammates were ready to lift him up onto their shoulders, but he waved them aside. He only had eyes for Rebecca Thompson. He ran right to her and grabbed her by the waist, picking her up and whirling her through the air. He even kissed her, right in front of everyone.

After the game was over, as the Hudson Falls team returned to the locker room, tired and triumphant, Josh and Rebecca strolled off arm in arm. They would spend hours together, talking and hugging, never getting enough of each other's company. He was the only guy for her, and she was the only girl for him. That's the way it was. . . .

Well, not *exactly*. Rebecca Thompson sighed, first with regret and then in exasperation, as she tugged a comb unsuccessfully through her thick, tangled wet hair. She had just taken a long, hot shower that had washed the dust of the baseball field off her body, but hadn't managed to wash away the embarrassment of the scene she had just lived through.

The part about the baseball game was true at least. Josh Kramer was a hero, and Rebecca and her best friend, Kathy McBride, had cheered themselves hoarse for him and, as an afterthought, for Rebecca's twin brother, Eric, and the rest of the Hudson Falls team. Rebecca's left ear was still ringing from Kathy screaming, "Isn't he amazing?" into it.

Rebecca had been too breathless to answer out loud, but inside she had agreed silently that he was amazing. At the end of the game Kathy had grabbed her hand and they swarmed onto the field with everyone else to congratulate the team. *That* much was true, too. And Rebecca had been wearing a denim skirt and her new jade green cotton sweater, but she hadn't felt beautiful and provocative at all. She had felt plain. As for her hair, it had not been even close to smooth—she had had to pinch it back into a tight french braid to subdue it.

In fact, Rebecca hadn't even wanted to speak to the players after the game. But Kathy knew just about every guy on the team and wouldn't have dreamed of leaving without telling each and every one what a great game he had played.

So Rebecca had found herself milling about with dozens of other students. Kathy and

Rebecca bumped into Eric, and Rebecca noticed him shoot an admiring glance at Kathy. It wasn't surprising. With her tall, slim figure and long blond hair, Kathy was definitely eye-catching.

Then Rebecca had lost Kathy in the crowd and suddenly found herself face to face with Josh Kramer himself. And if he was amazing when viewed from a distance, he was absolutely incredible from a few inches away.

Josh gave Rebecca a friendly "hello" as he had done dozens of times before. He played a lot of sports with Eric and the two boys were pretty good friends, so Josh's path crossed Rebecca's regularly. And just as *she* had done dozens of times before, Rebecca whispered "hi" in a tiny voice. Then, as she had stood staring hopelessly into Josh's unbelievably gorgeous gray eyes, one of her contact lenses popped out and disappeared into the dirt.

Josh had looked astonished as Rebecca clutched her eye, then dropped to her hands and knees and began pawing at the pitcher's mound.

"Need some help?" he had asked in a deep voice. Rebecca racked her brain for some light, amusing answer. If she were Kathy she would have known just the right thing to say. But nothing had come to her. She might as well have lost her voice as well as her lens.

Josh had gotten down on his hands and

knees to help. They had bumped heads, and immediately Rebecca's cheeks caught fire. She abandoned her search for the lens, mumbled her thanks to Josh, and darted away. Another opportunity, another chance to get to know him, lost. . . .

Rebecca sighed and tossed her comb into the sink with disgust. She wiped the fogged-up mirror with the back of her hand and stared at her reflection as if she expected to see the words "You blew it" written across her face.

Instead she saw a pair of soft green eyes, behind the glasses she'd worn until eighth grade when she had gotten contacts, a short freckled nose, a small but pretty mouth, and lots—*lots*—of wet, wavy brown hair.

Rebecca leaned forward and puffed a breath at the mirror to fog it back up. Sometimes she thought her face was kind of pretty, but that was not one of those times. She thought that being cute might someday make up for the fact that she was probably the shyest person in the world. But after that afternoon it looked as if the scale would be irreversibly tipped in favor of all-conquering shyness. She decided that she might as well flush the other contact lens down the toilet for all the good it would do her! Her nerdy old glasses would only proclaim to the world what it already knew—Rebecca Thompson was shy, studious, and serious. All the things the popular kids at Hudson Falls High weren't.

From the moment he had come to Hudson Falls High Josh became the king of the popular crowd. It was true he wasn't conceited, Rebecca thought, although with all the attention he got he probably should have been. Even on the baseball team he didn't hog the spotlight. He maintained as low a profile as his outstanding athletic ability would allow, and the other guys liked him for it. Rebecca had a class with him, and she knew he was smart but he didn't flaunt his intelligence, either.

All in all he was almost too perfect, but his sense of humor always saved him from being a plastic mannequin. To top it off, Josh Kramer had mystique. He could have dated any girl in school, but he had only gone out with a few of the prettiest, and those only a couple of times each.

Everyone thought they knew the reason why he dated so rarely, though. Rumor had it that when he had lived in New York City, Josh went out with Monica DeForest, the sixteen-year-old super model, whose picture appeared regularly in magazines. But when his family had moved to Hudson Falls their relationship ended. Supposedly he didn't talk about it much, even to a friend like Eric Thompson. But it was fairly obvious to Rebecca that he was searching for a substitute for Monica by dating Shannon Daly and Julie Stevenson who *looked* like models.

It was clear to Rebecca what kind of girl Josh Kramer was attracted to, and she knew she didn't have the knockout looks or personality to win him over.

Rebecca reached below the sink for the blow dryer. Her half-damp hair had already begun to curl; there wasn't a moment to lose. In her ongoing battle against the frizzies, it was kill or be killed.

"Becky! Can we come in a minute?"

Rebecca heard her mother's voice above the roar of the dryer. She turned it off and opened the bathroom door. Mrs. Thompson stood in the hallway holding Rebecca's four-year-old sister, Melissa, at arm's length. Melissa's hands, face, and overalls were covered with chocolate.

"Melissa, look at you!" Rebecca said playfully. "What have you been into?"

"A big bowl of icing." Mrs. Thompson rolled her eyes and laughed. Rebecca stepped aside, and her mother deposited Melissa in the tub and started unbuckling her overalls. "We made a devil's food cake for the bake sale at her nursery school tomorrow."

"I licked the bowl, Becky," Melissa said proudly.

"I bet you were a real help!"

"I think you'll agree this calls for a bath, Becky." Mrs. Thompson bent over to put the stopper in the tub. "Sorry to horn in on you like this. Are you finished in here?"

"Pretty much," Rebecca said. "I can finish my hair in my room." She pointed to a smudge of chocolate on her mother's face and shook her head. "I don't know, Mom. Looks like Melissa's not the only one who licked the bowl!"

Mrs. Thompson looked sheepish. The doorbell rang downstairs. "What timing!" Mrs. Thompson muttered.

"Eric will answer it," Rebecca said.

"No, he's out back, putting the finishing touches on his miniature golf course. He's oblivious to anything else." Mrs. Thompson stood up and wiped her hands on her pants. "I'll get the door. Will you start Melissa's bath for me? Thanks."

Rebecca looked at her little sister and wondered how she had managed to get icing *under* her overalls. Rebecca sighed. Soaping and shampooing Melissa would take both hands. Her own hair would have to wait.

A couple of minutes later Eric's voice echoed up through the open bathroom window from the backyard.

"Okay, Josh! Let's see what you're made of on the golf course."

Rebecca lifted her head with a jerk and peeked out the window over the tub. Josh Kramer was on the patio talking to her brother.

Rebecca gulped, then looked down at Melissa just in time to see her rub her eye with soapy fingers.

"Melissa, watch out!" It was too late. Her sister was already crying. Rebecca grabbed a washcloth and tried to rinse out Melissa's eye. Melissa squirmed and hollered. Rebecca groaned. Where was her mom when she needed her? Josh was in her backyard, and here *she* was, dressed in her bathrobe, her hair beyond rescue!

"I'm sorry I took so long, Becky." Mrs. Thompson flew into the bathroom. "As soon as I answered the door the phone rang. I'll take over now, honey."

"Thanks, Mom." Rebecca grabbed the blow dryer and raced out of the bathroom and down the hall. Shutting the door to her room behind her, she went to the window and cautiously pushed the curtains aside.

The yard behind her family's colonial house sloped steeply down toward a field and beyond that to a stand of pine trees. Eric and Josh were now on the other side of the vegetable garden at the bottom of the hill.

Rebecca's heart fluttered. Josh Kramer was in her own backyard! Maybe she was being given another chance after she had blown it at the baseball game. Or maybe she was getting another chance to make a fool of herself. Well, she had to risk it.

There wasn't any point in using the dryer now; Rebecca's hair had dried in a cloud of wild curls. She wrinkled her nose in disgust. Nothing for it but The Barrette. She grabbed her mass of hair in both hands and twisted it into a knot, clipping it back. She dressed quickly in khaki bermuda shorts and a blue polo shirt.

Rebecca raced out of her room, down to the back door, and out onto the patio, pausing to take one deep breath.

On the miniature golf course, Josh was trying to make a shot between two bags of peat moss, and Eric was watching him intently.

Rebecca walked slowly down the steps from the patio, then stopped, glued to the lawn like a statue. *Suppose they don't want me down there?* she thought, shoving her hands deep into the pockets of her shorts. *I'll probably just be in the way.* She squinted to better focus on Josh, and what she saw made her knees wobble—as usual. His sunny blond hair had fallen over his eyes as he bent forward to make the shot, and his tanned arms looked muscular and strong.

Rebecca felt her throat grow tight—a sure sign that an attack of shyness was on its way. But she fought against it. After all, her shyness was nothing new. She had always been shy around guys, doubly so around guys she liked. She had had crushes on boys before that had never come to anything, but she wanted this one to be different. She could tell Josh was something special.

She clenched her teeth with determination. "Here goes nothing!"

As she started down the hill, Eric peeked out from behind the apple tree. "Becky! Come on down! I want you to try out my golf course. Unless you're afraid of the competition."

Rebecca laughed. "Yeah, you guys look like you're ready for the U.S. Open!" She wished she felt as lighthearted as she sounded. Her flip-flops might as well have been made of concrete as she strode down the hill.

"Hi, Rebecca," Josh said when she joined them. "What do you think of the course?"

Rebecca felt her face grow pink at the sound of his voice. She grimaced inwardly. If *she'd* been in charge of creating the human race, she would *not* have invented the blush. At least she would have made it optional, like a tape deck in a car. She looked into Josh's eyes and turned even pinker.

"It's great," she said as casually as she could. "You look like you play pretty well. But not as well as you play baseball—I mean, you play baseball *really* well. I mean, congratulations on winning the game!" Rebecca was amazed that anyone could sound as stupid as she did.

"Thanks!" Josh smiled and seemed to be genuinely pleased at the compliment.

Rebecca tingled. Josh hadn't laughed at her. He hadn't turned away from her, bored. What was more, she thought, he'd called her "Rebecca." Suddenly she remembered the day she and Josh had met.

It was just a few days after her sixteenth birthday. Her brother and Josh were already friends, but most of the time they spent together was in the gym or on an athletic field. Josh didn't come over just to *talk* to Eric the way Kathy came over to talk to Rebecca. And the few times he had stopped by the house, she hadn't been around.

On that afternoon she was on her way to a guitar lesson. She was late, so she took the stairs in two giant bounds, her guitar case flapping against her leg. She landed at the bottom—*thump!*—just as her brother and Josh came in the front door loaded down with ice-hockey gear. Needless to say, there had been a head-on collision—everything and everyone went flying.

The boys laughed. Rebecca wanted to cry, but managed to maintain her composure. As he gathered up his scattered skates and gloves, Josh had said, "You must be Eric's twin sister. I've seen you around, but no one's bothered to introduce us. I'm Josh Kramer."

As if she didn't know! She had "seen him around," too. In fact, she had been spending all of her spare time daydreaming about what it would be like to actually meet him.

She never could have imagined *that* meeting, though. She had managed to croak out, "My name's Rebecca." Then she quickly had taken his outstretched hand to shake it just as she realized she was still clutching a handful of guitar picks. Josh's gray eyes had opened wide with surprise. "Better than one of those trick palm buzzers!" he had observed with a broad grin. Rebecca had been glad to rush off to her lesson.

Recalling that first encounter brought back all the embarrassment that came with it, and also reminded Rebecca of their second close encounter—that very day at the baseball game. It was only too clear what Josh must think of her, no matter how polite he sounded.

Rebecca suddenly realized she had been staring at Josh the whole time she'd been thinking. He was staring right back at her with a curious expression in his eyes. Before she could turn around and run back up the hill, where she planned to stay in her room for the rest of her life, Eric saved the day.

"Can we get on with the game?" Eric

had just shot and was twirling his club impatiently.

Josh took another shot. Rebecca felt instantly better, now that the focus was off her and back on golf. The ball rolled neatly and landed in a plastic yogurt container that had been sunk into the ground under the apple tree.

"Hole in one!" Eric shouted.

Josh smiled and waved at the applause of an imaginary crowd as he strolled toward the tree to collect his golf ball. Rebecca couldn't help but giggle.

Eric whistled and shook his head. "That's going to be a tough shot to follow. I think I need to take a break to quench my thirst. How about a soda?"

"I'd love one," Josh said.

"What about you, Becky?"

Rebecca felt her mouth go dry with nervousness. She was going to be left alone with Josh while Eric got the sodas. "Sure. Thanks, Eric," she said in a squeaky voice.

Eric jogged up to the house. Josh stood looking at Rebecca, and Rebecca stood looking down at the lawn. It seemed to be forever to her before she made herself raise her head and return his gaze.

"So . . ." she finally said, her voice trailing off feebly.

"So . . ." he said, echoing her. They stood

in silence for a few more minutes. "Why don't we play some golf?"

Rebecca shrugged. "I'm not very good at sports," she said. "Eric's the jock in the family. Not that miniature golf is much of a sport, but you know what I mean."

"That's right. You're a musician," Josh replied. "How's the guitar going?"

Rebecca looked blank. "The guitar?"

"You were heading for a lesson the last time I bumped into you here," Josh said. "I assume that means you play the guitar." He propped his club on the ground and leaned forward on it, a spark of interest in his eyes. "I've been meaning to ask you about that."

Rebecca was stunned at the thought that Josh could be interested in something she did.

"Yeah," he continued before she could say anything, "I love the guitar! I think a good guitarist makes a band great, don't you?" He reeled off a half-dozen names, none of whom Rebecca recognized, even though one of them was, in Josh's opinion at least, "the greatest rock guitarist that ever lived."

"Oh," she said lamely. "I don't play *that* kind of guitar." She pretended to study a leaf on the apple tree. "I'm learning classical and folk guitar."

She wasn't sure if Josh was disappointed or not. If he was, he didn't say so. "That's

15

cool!" He smiled. "I'm impressed. I love any kind of music, but I'm not too musical myself."

There was a pause. Rebecca knew she should say something next. That was the rule of conversation—you took turns. Why did she find that so hard? "Um—let's try the golf course!" If they were playing, they wouldn't have to talk, she realized.

"Great!" Josh said. "I know just the hole we should try first!"

They walked together to the clump of pine trees where Eric had placed one end of a wooden board against a stack of bricks to make a ramp.

"You have to hit the ball up the plank and try to get it in the bucket." Josh crossed his arms across his broad chest. "You go first."

Rebecca put her ball on the ground and aimed in the general direction of the board. The ball hopped unevenly up the ramp and missed the bucket by yards. "I'm just not good at this," she said apologetically.

"Take it over," Josh said kindly, retrieving the ball and dropping it at her feet.

This time the ball avoided the wooden board entirely, choosing to hit the trunk of a pine tree instead.

Josh raised one sun-bleached eyebrow. "Have you ever played miniature golf before?" he asked doubtfully.

Rebecca felt trapped. She was never going

to make a good impression on Josh if it depended on her golfing skill. "Only once or twice," she admitted. "It's Eric's miniature golf course, not mine." Rebecca heard the defensive note in her voice. Josh must have heard it, too.

"Hey," he said with a smile that was casual but warm, "no problem. Don't be so hard on yourself." Rebecca looked away shyly. "You can't expect to be great at something you've hardly ever done." She looked up at him, her head tipped to one side. Josh put a hand lightly on her shoulder. His touch was warm even through her shirt. "It's like your guitar, or my baseball," he said, continuing. "You've got to practice, that's all. A little coaching never hurt, either. Here, let me help you with your swing."

Before Rebecca knew what was happening, Josh was standing behind her, his arms around her, his hands positioning hers on the golf club. Rebecca felt herself tense up, but Josh didn't seem to share her discomfort. With Josh's gentle guidance she swung the club and hit the ball. It rolled easily up the plank and landed with a *thunk* in the pail.

"Hey, look what I did!" Rebecca was thrilled. "I'm not so bad after all!"

"Of course not—you're fantastic." Josh looked amused. "See, all you need is a little

17

practice." He walked over to the pail and leaned over to pluck out the golf ball. "You'll be beating Eric soon."

Rebecca laughed. "That would be worth all the practice in the world," she said. "I wish he'd seen the shot we just made together."

"I think he might have." Josh nodded up the hill. Eric was looking down at them, holding three cans of soda.

Rebecca suddenly felt flustered. Josh had returned to her side with the ball, but she quickly moved a few feet off. How had she had the nerve to let Josh Kramer coach her at miniature golf? It was crazy—she was much too shy.

And from the way Josh walked quickly up the hill to meet her brother, she thought he must have been eager to go. He probably felt he had already wasted enough time on his friend's twin sister. Rebecca swallowed her disappointment and followed him.

Josh and Eric were talking about the baseball game when she joined them. Once again, Rebecca felt on the outside of things. Her moment of togetherness with Josh was over. Maybe it hadn't meant anything to begin with. After all, she thought, what had really happened? Nothing. At least, nothing from Josh's point of view. He probably gave miniature golf lessons to girls every day, to poised, glamorous models who weren't wearing bermuda shorts and didn't get nervous just being near a boy.

"Why don't you stay for dinner?" Eric asked Josh after they had sat and talked awhile.

Rebecca's heart leaped and then fell.

"No, I'd better get moving," said Josh. "Thanks, anyway."

"Sure," said Eric. "I'll walk you to your car."

Rebecca pretended to be absorbed in looking at the daisies bordering the patio.

"So long, Rebecca," Josh called.

She looked up at him and said as if it were an afterthought, "Oh, 'bye, Josh." She watched the two boys disappear around the side of the house. There was no doubt about it, she thought. Josh Kramer was wonderful in every way. It wasn't just his looks, although those were great. He was fun and he was thoughtful, and he radiated complete confidence.

Rebecca wasn't quite sure what to think about Josh and herself now. Maybe, just maybe, she was ready to laugh about the contact lens fiasco. She had had another chance with Josh, and it hadn't been a *total* loss.

The contact lens fiasco! Rebecca's hands flew to her face and felt the unmistakable plastic of her eighth grade glasses. *Oh, no,* she thought, horrified. *Oh, no! No wonder Josh looked at me kind of funny—it's a won-*

der he looked at me at all! Between the glasses and the hairstyle . . . She yanked the barrette out of her hair and glared at it. I must have made a great picture. A good story to tell the guys on the baseball team when my brother's not around!

Chapter Two

Rebecca stood at the kitchen counter slicing a cucumber. She was still excited about having seen Josh and was bursting to talk about it to somebody. She glanced at her mother. Mrs. Thompson met her daughter's eye and smiled as she stuffed some freshly cooked carrots into the food processor. Rebecca opened her mouth to speak but smiled back instead. The noisy food processor made it impossible to talk. She wasn't ready to confess to her mom, anyway. She'd wait until she spoke to Kathy.

Just then the telephone rang. Rebecca grabbed it. "Hello?"

"Becky, you won't believe what happened to me this afternoon!" Kathy said in a breathless rush on the other end of the line.

"Well, *you* won't believe—" Rebecca looked

over at her mother, who was emptying the pureed carrots into a pan. She put her hand over the mouthpiece of the phone. "Mom, do I have five minutes?"

"Sure," Mrs. Thompson answered. "The chicken's not quite done, so go ahead."

Rebecca pulled the receiver into the hall for privacy. "Kathy, wait until you hear—" she said.

"No, me first!" Kathy said, interrupting. "Guess who I'm going to the movies with Saturday night?"

"You've got me." Rebecca laughed. "It could be one of a hundred people!"

"Well, then I'll tell you. Kenny Schmidt!" Kathy's tone was rapturous.

"Kenny Schmidt? The biggest brain in school? He's more of a nerd than I am!" Rebecca was astounded.

"Never mind his brain," Kathy said. "I like his muscles."

"I guess he *is* good-looking," Rebecca said after a moment's thought. "But he's so shy. How did you ever get him to ask you out?"

"I didn't. *I* asked him out."

"*You* asked *him*?" Rebecca asked in amazement.

"That's right," said Kathy. "He's shy. So, I figured he needed a little encouragement. There we were at the library—"

"The library?"

"Sure! He was there when I went by after the game to return some overdue books, and we ended up studying together," Kathy said, explaining.

"*You?* Studying on a Friday afternoon?" Rebecca hooted.

"I wasn't *really* studying, Becky. I was *pretending* to study. Understand?"

"Yeah." Rebecca leaned against the wall and slid down it until she was sitting on the floor. "I get the picture."

"So," Kathy said, "I simply popped the question."

Rebecca shook her head in admiration. "Wow, that really takes nerve."

"I know, but look where a little nerve'll get you!" Kathy laughed. "So what's *your* news?"

"Well—Josh Kramer was at my house this afternoon!"

"No way!" Kathy shrieked. "And I thought I was lucky! What happened? Did you speak to him? Did he speak to you?"

"Yes," Rebecca admitted. "We talked. He seems like such a nice guy—"

"No kidding!" Kathy gasped, cutting in. "He's Mr. Wonderful. Everybody knows *that*."

"I just wish I had half the nerve you do, Kath."

"You mean with boys?" Kathy asked sympathetically.

"Yes," Rebecca groaned. "It's the same old

story. I blush. I get tongue-tied. I feel like I have four left feet. There I was with Josh Kramer and I just couldn't find anything to say. I mean outside of the ordinary. 'Hi. How are you? Nice weather we're having.' That kind of stuff."

"Well, talking isn't everything, you know," Kathy said. "The best way to get to know a guy is to do things with him."

"We did play miniature golf, but—"

"Great!" Kathy said, sounding like the head cheerleader at a pep rally. "That's a good start. It would definitely be a plus to learn about baseball, too, since sports are his big thing."

"Well, sports might be his big thing, but they're certainly not mine." Rebecca twirled the phone cord around her finger, feeling discouraged.

"There must be other things you have in common," Kathy said reassuringly.

"I'm not so certain."

Kathy heard the catch in Rebecca's voice. "This is more than just a little crush, isn't it, Becky?"

Rebecca sighed deeply. "Yeah. I think this is for real."

"Well, you've just got to get in there and fight, that's all," Kathy said matter-of-factly.

"But how?" Rebecca asked, frustrated. "That's easy for *you* to say. You never have trouble talking to boys. But for me—"

Just then Mrs. Thompson called from the kitchen. "Becky. Dinner's ready!"

"Okay, I'm coming!" Rebecca said. "Kathy, I've got to go."

"Look, Becky, don't let this thing with Josh get you down. I'm sure you'll find some way of getting him to realize that you're made for each other."

Rebecca smiled. "Thanks, Kath. That helps. I just wish I had a new personality or something."

Kathy laughed. "There's absolutely nothing wrong with your personality. I've always kind of liked it. Now your wardrobe . . ."

"You're bad, Kathy McBride! Just because I don't own tiger-striped tights in five different neon colors!"

"Hey, don't knock it! Creative dressing happens to be the key to the real me."

Rebecca giggled. "I've really got to go. I'll talk to you tomorrow."

"See you, Becky."

Rebecca said goodbye and turned toward the kitchen, almost colliding with Eric.

"Who were you talking to?" he asked casually.

"Just Kathy," Rebecca said. She looked at him suspiciously. "Eric! Were you eavesdropping?"

"Of course!" He nodded and then winked. "But relax," he said. "I just heard the last part. I missed the stuff about who you have a crush on."

Rebecca's stomach bounced with butterflies. She wondered how much of the conversation Eric had really heard. He sounded as if he knew everything.

"So you like the golf course, huh?" Eric asked, changing the subject as they walked into the kitchen.

"Well, it's as weird as you are," Rebecca said casually. "But it's fun. Maybe I'll give it another try tomorrow. You could give me a few pointers."

"Absolutely, Becky. After a few lessons from me you'll be good enough to beat Josh."

Rebecca narrowed her eyes at her brother. He looked innocent enough, but she knew him too well to be fooled. And she guessed he knew *her* too well not to have noticed the way she was acting that afternoon when Josh was over.

Rebecca and Eric took their places at the table. Rebecca tried to catch her brother's eye to let him know she was interested in renewing their conversation after dinner. He ignored her signals.

"Too bad Josh couldn't stay for dinner," Mr. Thompson said. The comment was directed at Eric, but Rebecca's ears perked up. "He seems so nice."

"Yeah, Josh is great," Eric said, biting into a drumstick.

"You should bring him around more often." Mrs. Thompson laughed. "He's your only friend who doesn't eat us out of house and home when he comes over."

Rebecca pushed some salad around her plate, trying not to appear *too* interested in the topic of conversation.

Her mother observed that Josh seemed to keep to himself a lot.

"It's true," Eric said. "I think he still misses his old high school."

"That's natural," Mr. Thompson said.

Eric nodded and threw a knowing look at Rebecca. "I'm pretty sure there's a girl involved, too."

"A girl?" she asked in what she hoped was a casual manner.

"Yeah. He has a picture of her in his locker. She must be his girlfriend from his old school. They broke up, I know that much, but I think he still thinks about her—a lot."

Rebecca lost what little appetite she had had. She pictured an eight-by-ten glossy photograph of Monica DeForest smiling out from Josh's locker. She stared at her plate, reminding herself not to jump to conclusions. Sure, everyone at school was positive that Josh had dated Monica DeForest, but Eric must have seen the photograph. And if it were Monica DeForest, wouldn't he have said so? Rebecca suddenly felt encouraged.

Mr. Thompson interrupted Rebecca's thoughts. "What do you think, Helen? Is it time to let them in on our secret?"

"Sure. I think now is the perfect time." She smiled at her children and winked at her husband.

Rebecca couldn't help feeling excited. "What's it about?"

"It's about our vacation," Mr. Thompson said, pausing for dramatic effect.

"Are we going to the beach again, Dad?" Rebecca asked.

"We're going to the mountains, this time," her father replied.

"The Adirondacks?" Eric said, guessing.

"Not exactly." Mr. Thompson took a deliberate bite of his chicken and chewed it slowly. "We're going to the Rockies!"

Eric and Rebecca both gasped. Melissa looked at her older brother and sister and let her small mouth drop open in imitation of theirs.

The Rockies were much farther than they had ever gone for a vacation. To Rebecca, the Rockies sounded as distant and exotic as the Alps.

"How did you swing that, Dad?" Eric asked.

"This summer the Newspaper Editors Conference is being held in Calgary, Alberta, at the foot of the Canadian Rockies. We've got a reservation for three weeks at a place called the Kicking Horse Ranch, about an hour from the city. Sound fun?"

"Fantastic!" shouted Eric.

"I can't wait!" said Rebecca.

"Yay!" sang out Melissa, sticking a finger into her pureed carrots for emphasis.

"When do we leave?" Eric asked.

"In two weeks, right after school gets out."

"Will we have a chance to ride, Dad?" Rebecca asked. She had taken lessons when she was younger and always wanted a horse of her own. She was thrilled at the prospect of riding again.

"We sure will," he answered.

Mrs. Thompson was smiling at her family's enthusiasm. "Your father and I thought you two older kids might each like to invite a friend along. We're driving out and back so it won't be too expensive."

Eric let out a whoop of delight.

"That's the greatest idea," Rebecca exclaimed. She was already imagining the call she'd make to Kathy, right after dinner. "This vacation is going to be terrific!"

Her parents looked pleased. Rebecca knew they looked forward to family trips as much as she and her brother and sister did. It suddenly occurred to her what this trip would mean, though. With the traveling time, it would be four weeks away from home—away from Josh. He'd forget she ever existed. He'd start a summer romance with someone else, or worse, he'd get back with Monica the Model.

"I know who I'm going to invite!" Eric announced. "Josh! I was thinking that I'd miss him once baseball season was over."

"That's a wonderful idea, Eric," said Mrs. Thompson. "I hope Josh's parents will let him go."

Rebecca was stunned. She didn't know whether to shriek with delight or faint. Hundreds of images flashed through her mind at once—mountains, streams, horses, sunshine, her guitar, and Josh. She pictured Josh in a cowboy hat, Josh galloping across a field, Josh holding her in his arms. It would be like a movie. She couldn't believe her good luck.

She was ecstatic, and at the same time terrified. For four weeks she would be seeing Josh every day. What would she wear? How would she act? She could hardly get up the nerve to speak to him in her own backyard. What would she say to him for three weeks in the Canadian Rockies, to say nothing of the time spent traveling there?

Suddenly a hand appeared before her eyes.

"Earth to Becky!" Eric was waving in front of her face. "Who are you going to take on the trip?"

"Oh! I'm going to ask Kathy, obviously."

"Great!" Eric looked pleased. "Kathy always livens things up."

Rebecca nodded her head absentmindedly. She had hardly heard her brother. She was already on top of a mountain—with Josh, the boy of her dreams.

Rebecca called Kathy at the earliest possible moment, and, as she had expected, her friend was as enthusiastic about the trip as she was.

"No way! This is outrageous!" Kathy shrieked. Before Rebecca could tell her the part about Josh, Kathy had dropped the phone to run and ask her parents if she could take the trip. When she came back on the line, Kathy squealed, "I can go." The two girls shouted and jumped up and down. Rebecca then plunged into the dream-come-true story of Josh's going with them. He had accepted Eric's invitation five minutes earlier.

"What could be better?" Kathy asked. "Just imagine the two of you, strolling hand in hand under the moonlight, which has to be much more romantic in Canada than it is in Hudson Falls!"

"I know, I know," Rebecca said. "Believe me, my imagination's been running overtime. But it's all for nothing, Kath." She told her friend what Eric had said about the picture in Josh's locker and everything it might signify.

"But the picture's of an *ex*-girlfriend, and besides, she's in New York City and you're here. The odds are on your side. You've just got to go for it," Kathy argued.

"I don't know," said Rebecca. "Even if she—whoever she is—lived in Siberia, how could he possibly like me? I'll only make a fool of myself trying to let him know I'm interested. You know me, Kath. I'll never in a million years get up the nerve."

"Yeah, I know you." Kathy giggled. "So, a flirt you're not! Not everybody has the knack." Rebecca bristled and Kathy seemed to sense it. "But, hey, that's okay. We'll just do what we can to make all this easier for you."

"Like what?"

"I'm not sure yet," Kathy said. "Just give me some time. Speaking of which, I've got to go and figure out what to wear for my date with Kenny."

The girls said goodbye and Rebecca hung up the phone thinking back to another recent conversation with Kathy. She had experienced what she considered to be a catastrophe—she was seen by Josh having lunch in the cafeteria with Len Seaver, who was one of the school intellectuals and a real drip. Rebecca had gone out with Len once and was relieved that he'd never asked for a second date.

Kathy had put on her I-know-more-about-this-sort-of-thing-than-you-do face. "It's good public relations for Josh to see you with another boy," she had pointed out. "It'll remind him that you go out on dates. That can't hurt, can it?"

Rebecca had snorted. "You think it helps to remind him that I went out with someone like Len Seaver? That'll really make Josh want to join the I've-Dated-Rebecca-Thompson Club!"

Now she sighed. It looked hopeless.

Chapter Three

"You really think this will work, Kathy?" Rebecca reached up to feel the large rollers on her head with a doubtful expression on her face.

"Trust me," Kathy said as she continued to dry Rebecca's hair. "My mom has curly hair like yours, and this is the way she straightens it."

School was over for the year and the big vacation was only a few days away. Kathy had come over to Rebecca's to talk about clothes for the trip, and now they were experimenting with hairstyles. Rebecca, wearing her bathrobe, was perched on the edge of her old-fashioned, four-poster bed, and Kathy, in a white miniskirt and an orange tank top knelt behind her drying her hair. Hairpins and rollers were scattered all over the pale yellow bedspread.

"There, I'm done," Kathy announced, surveying her work with pride. "But don't take them out yet. Let it cool off first."

Rebecca stood up gingerly and walked over to the mirror. Her eyes widened. "Boy, do I look scary! And I thought my hair didn't need any help to look horrible. Josh should see me now! How come you used so many rollers?"

"Because your hair is so thick." Kathy slid off the bed and stood behind Rebecca, looking over her shoulder to meet her friend's eyes in the mirror. "It's like a horse's mane. Not that I've ever *felt* a horse's mane. Each strand is as thick as a toothpick!"

Rebecca grimaced. "Don't remind me!"

"I didn't mean that as a criticism," Kathy said. "Sometimes I wish I had curly hair like yours."

"No, you don't," Rebecca said good-naturedly. "You know you have the prettiest hair in the world. It's like an ad for perfect hair. Admit it, mine's a disaster."

Kathy shook her head. "You know what your problem is, Becky? You just don't give yourself enough credit." She laughed. "Go ahead—you keep hating your hair and I'll keep liking it."

Rebecca walked over to the window and

looked out into the yard, so Kathy wouldn't see her expression. She knew her friend was just trying to be nice, but sometimes her compliments were hard to take. It seemed to Rebecca that Kathy had grown up overnight. One summer she was a skinny little girl like Rebecca, and the next she looked like a *Vogue* cover girl, while Rebecca had hardly changed at all. And Kathy was so sure of herself. As far as Rebecca could tell, Kathy had completely skipped the awkward in-between stage. It just wasn't fair.

Rebecca pushed the curtains aside and shoved her window open higher. She let her eye drift over the backyard. The miniature golf course was still spread out on the lawn, but Eric had been instructed by his parents to take it down that day and cut the grass before they left for vacation.

"Where's Eric?" Kathy asked suddenly.

"Supposedly he's getting gas for the lawn mower. But he's been gone for hours."

"Too bad," said Kathy, helping herself to some mascara from Rebecca's makeup bag.

"I thought you thought Eric was boring," Rebecca said.

"Did I say that?" Kathy sounded surprised. "Well, maybe I used to think that. Lately, I've been thinking he's sort of fun." She generously applied mascara to her long lashes, darting a devilish smile at Rebecca.

Rebecca narrowed her eyes suspiciously. Kathy had cast aside Kenny Schmidt very quickly. "Don't tell me you've got a crush on Eric now!"

Kathy collapsed onto the bed. " 'Crush' isn't exactly the word for it. Let's just say I've discovered that I like talking to him. He makes me laugh. I want to get to know him better, that's all."

"But you already know him," Rebecca said, pointing out the obvious. "You've known him for years!"

"That was when we were kids," Kathy said. "Now things are different, and Eric's different, too."

"When it comes to boys, I'll never understand you, Kathy," Rebecca said with a wry smile.

"Don't get me wrong, Becky. Really. I couldn't be farther from having a crush on your brother. But I figure you'll be spending so much time with Josh that I'll be stuck with Eric whether I like it or not!"

Kathy grinned teasingly, but Rebecca didn't take the bait. Instead she marched abruptly to her dresser. "Let's go over the clothes. Want me to show you what I'm going to take?"

"Sure," said Kathy in a perplexed tone. "Is something wrong, Becky? Did I say something?"

Rebecca bent down and began sifting through the dresser drawers. "No, it's nothing you said," she mumbled. "It's just that—well, I think I should just forget about Josh."

"How can you forget about him when you're going on a vacation with him?"

"Very easily," said Rebecca, throwing an armful of clothes onto the bed.

"Why are you acting this way, Becky? Did something happen between you and Josh that you didn't tell me about?" Kathy's blue eyes were warm with concern.

"That's just it," said Rebecca. "Nothing happened. And nothing ever will!" Rebecca sat down on the bed, a red T-shirt in her hand, and sighed. "There's no point in my continuing to daydream about Josh, Kathy. He's never going to go for someone like me."

"Come on, Becky. Don't have such a bad attitude. Remember the way you told me he put his arms around you when he was teaching you golf?"

"Yeah, I remember," Rebecca said. "But that was a couple of weeks ago. Josh hasn't really talked to me since then. If he liked me—even a little bit—don't you think he'd try a little harder?"

"Maybe he's just been distracted," Kathy said reasonably. "There was the end of baseball season and finals and—"

"You know those aren't real excuses, Kath!" Rebecca said, cutting her off.

Kathy thought for a moment and then her face brightened. "Didn't he talk to you at the baseball victory celebration the other night? I thought I saw the two of you in a corner."

Rebecca turned the red T-shirt inside out and then back again. "I said 'congratulations' and he said 'thanks.' That was the extent of our conversation. I couldn't think of anything else to say. Besides, you saw the swarm of girls around him. I didn't stand a chance."

"You *do* stand a chance," Kathy said firmly. "Those girls might swarm around him, but Josh isn't dating any of them. I know that for a fact. I investigated it for you. Don't worry, I didn't ask Josh or even Eric. I have other sources."

Rebecca raised an eyebrow. "Are you sure?"

Kathy nodded. "Yep. Josh is available."

Rebecca let out a sigh of relative relief. "Thanks, Kath." She focused on the shirt she was holding. "Let's go over the clothes, okay?"

The girls stood up from the bed and looked at the pile of blue jeans, shorts, and shirts they had been sitting on.

Kathy picked through the clothes. "You don't have anything dressy in here."

Rebecca went over to her closet and looked inside. It wasn't an inspiring sight. "Really, Kathy, I think it's mostly going to be jeans."

"Jeans aren't the way to a man's heart." Kathy joined Rebecca by the closet. "You're not going to be horseback riding the whole time. Don't you ever think about how what you're wearing impresses other people?"

Rebecca shrugged. "Well, sure. I mean, sometimes I wear a dress and sometimes I don't. When I wear a dress I figure I look— dressy."

Kathy hit her forehead with the palm of her hand. "No, no, no! You've got it all wrong, Becky. Your clothes have to make more of a statement than that or guys you meet, like Josh Kramer, will think that's all there is to you—a conservative girl in conservative clothes."

"But maybe that's what I am," Rebecca said, defending herself indignantly. "What's so bad about that?"

"Absolutely nothing, but you yourself said you're worried you have an unglamorous image, and that's something you can change if you want. If you care about clothes they can help bring out the real you."

Rebecca giggled. "How can you say something like that with a serious face?"

"Because I am serious. Look, I'll prove it to you. What do you think the secret of my success with boys is?"

"Don't fish for compliments from me, Kathy McBride!"

"I'm not, I'm trying to make a point." Kathy gave Rebecca a playful shove. "Okay, I'll tell you my secret, since you asked. It's my wardrobe!"

Rebecca groaned.

"I kid you not. I wear clothes that make me feel funky and wild, or soft and feminine, whatever's appropriate. And I always wear things that fit me inside so I feel relaxed. For example, what did you wear on your date with what's-his-name—Len Seaver? Do you remember?"

"I do, but I'd rather not," Rebecca said ruefully. "I think I wore my denim skirt and a turtleneck and sweater. It was winter."

"And how did that make you feel?" asked Kathy. She looked like a lawyer arguing a case before a jury.

"Terrible! I told you, it was the world's worst date."

"Well, forget that part. Did the way you were dressed make Len warm up to you at all?"

Rebecca frowned in distaste. "I didn't want him to!"

"What I'm *trying* to suggest, Becky, is that with the right clothes you can make a guy look at you twice, and want to get close to you." Kathy sounded slightly exasperated.

Rebecca had heard enough about clothes.

Kathy's theory only made the shortcomings of her own wardrobe more obvious. "Well, I'm just going to follow the list the ranch sent. Look, it says to bring a jacket because the nights get cool." Rebecca tossed a sheet of paper at Kathy, who glanced at it and sighed dreamily.

"I bet they have big campfires at night. Just think, Becky, there we'll be out under the stars. You and Josh—Oh, it's perfect!"

"Yeah, but will I be wearing the right thing?" Rebecca couldn't help joking.

"Oh, you!" Kathy threw a pillow at her.

Just then there was a knock at Rebecca's door. Eric stuck his head in and looked at his sister in amazement. "What happened to *you*?"

Rebecca instinctively reached up to feel her head—she had forgotten all about the rollers.

"We're playing beauty parlor," Kathy said. "Come on in!" She pulled Rebecca to a sitting position on the bed and began removing the rollers.

Eric watched for a while, amused. "Looks like you could have a career in hair, Kath."

Kathy whipped out the last roller and then brushed Rebecca's hair smooth. "All right, Becky. Check it out!"

Rebecca crossed to the mirror while Kathy and Eric looked on. Her hair *was* straighter.

She touched it experimentally. "It worked, Kathy," she said, suddenly feeling self-conscious.

Eric studied her seriously. "Are you sure that's really your hair, Beck? It doesn't look half bad!"

"Thanks for nothing!" Rebecca laughed.

As he was speaking, Eric had draped one arm casually around Kathy's shoulders. Rebecca couldn't help but notice how comfortable Kathy was with this gesture. She didn't blush or jump away or get tongue-tied as Rebecca would have in similar circumstances. Kathy could joke casually with Eric without losing a beat.

"But, hey," Eric exclaimed. "How about some golf? A farewell game, before I have to take down the course. Josh is downstairs, waiting—"

Rebecca and Kathy exchanged a shocked look. "Josh is here?" Rebecca asked, her voice shrill.

"Sure is," said Eric cheerfully. "You're lucky he didn't come up with me and catch you in your curlers. Well, what do you say?" Eric shifted his gaze from Rebecca to Kathy and let his eyes rest on her. "Will you two be joining us?"

"I don't know," Rebecca said.

"Of course we will," Kathy said decisively. "We'll be right down."

As soon as Eric left, Rebecca closed her bedroom door and looked at Kathy desperately. "Kathy, I can't see Josh now! I'm not even dressed, and my hair's not really done."

"It's all done, Becky, and it looks great. Here, try these gold combs I brought with me."

Rebecca took the combs and, brushing her hair back on either side, used them to pin it in place.

"You're beautiful, Becky," Kathy said sincerely.

"My hair could still be straighter," Rebecca said.

"Who cares?" Kathy waved a pink nail-polished hand. "I like it. Hurry up and throw on your favorite *jeans*—I'm going downstairs!"

Kathy disappeared, and Rebecca was left alone with her new hairstyle and her old shyness. She fished through her makeup bag for some peach-colored lipstick, the same color that Kathy was wearing, and quickly put it on. She pursed her lips and looked at her reflection in the mirror critically. Why didn't the lipstick have the same effect on her?

Just before she opened the back door to the patio, she stopped and said a silent prayer. *Please don't let me get tongue-tied this time. This time, please let me be—interesting.* She peeked timidly outside.

"Hi, Rebecca." Josh's deep voice made her jump.

Rebecca emerged slowly from the house. "Hey, how are you?"

"Oh, hanging in there." Josh's smile was friendly enough, but his words had a final quality that didn't encourage Rebecca to respond.

"Come on down!" It was a relief when Eric shouted up at them from the far end of the yard. "We're ready to start!"

Rebecca and Josh were both eager to join Eric and Kathy. They practically sprinted down the hill to the miniature golf course.

"Let's get on with this game, everybody!" Kathy shouted. "I'm in rare form today!" She playfully struck the pose of a baseball batter and took a fake swing with her golf club.

"Wrong sport, Kathy," Eric said kindly.

Kathy dropped the pose and feigned surprise. "It is?"

"But that's okay, you can play anything you want. We're liberal around here."

Josh and Rebecca were standing awkwardly side by side watching the other two clown around. Finally Josh cleared his throat loudly. "Um-mmm—how about starting? Are we going to play in teams?"

Rebecca blushed. Obviously Josh found the silence between them as uncomfortable as she did.

"That's what I'd planned," Eric said.

"Why don't you two be a team?" Josh suggested, pointing to Kathy and Eric. "You seem to have complementary styles."

Rebecca tried not to show her surprise. Eric hit his forehead in a fake show of dismay. "No way! Me, the miniature golf champ of the season, on the same team as someone who doesn't know the difference between a hole in one and a home run?"

Kathy lowered her eyes and gazed at Eric coolly, but her smile was warm. "I'm more than happy to take my diverse talents elsewhere, Bud."

"Great!" Eric winked at her. "Come on, Becky, I guess you're stuck with me."

Rebecca bit her lip. It would have been nice to be Josh's partner, but maybe she'd be safer with Eric. She'd have a slightly harder time making a fool of herself playing with her brother.

"All right, Eric," she said cheerfully. "I'll take the first shot, okay?" *Better to get it over with*, she thought. She was conscious of the other three watching her as she positioned her golf ball and began her swing. She wasn't comfortable being the center of attention, and she felt her arms shake as she lifted the club.

"Watch out for Rebecca!" Josh said suddenly in a loud whisper. "I taught her everything she knows."

Josh's teasing comment affected Rebecca like a lightning bolt. A surge of nervous energy shot through her, and she hit the ball with about twenty times the necessary force. It popped up in the air, sailed over the vegetable garden, and landed somewhere among the pines.

Eric shook his head in disbelief. "Becky, this is *miniature* golf—remember? You're not teeing off on some country club course!"

Kathy and Josh both laughed and Rebecca was mortified. "Sorry," she said in a small voice. "I don't know what came over me. I'll go find the ball."

The smell of pine needles greeted her at the edge of the grove. She scanned the grass that bordered the pines, but no golf ball. She got on her hands and knees and peered beneath the heavy boughs of the trees. *Well, with any luck it'll take me four weeks to find the thing,* she thought. *Everyone can go on vacation and come back without me along!*

"Kind of like an egg hunt, huh?" Josh said as he knelt beside her.

Rebecca felt another jolt of electricity. She jumped. "Yeah, an egg hunt," she said, searching for an inspiring comment. She crawled into the space beneath the trees and continued to look for the ball. *Egg hunt?* she thought desperately. *What am I supposed to say next?*

To Rebecca's dismay, Josh followed her, and for a long moment they crouched together on the soft carpet of pine needles in silence. Josh's face was so close to Rebecca's that she could hear his breathing. She hoped he couldn't hear her heart—it was pounding like a drum.

"Nice spot," Josh finally said conversationally.

"Beautiful," said Rebecca. "But no sign of the ball." She began to back out from under the trees.

"Wait!" Josh reached out and gripped her arm.

Rebecca's body tensed and her mouth went dry. She turned and stared at him. She gulped loudly. "What is it?"

"The ball." Josh pointed around the side of a rough-barked tree trunk. "There it is."

Rebecca sprang forward on her knees. "I'll get it!" Josh reached for it at the same time. They bumped heads even worse than the day after the baseball game.

"Ouch!" Rebecca exclaimed. "I mean, excuse me!"

"My fault," Josh said as he grinned and rubbed his own head. "I've got a hard head. I don't really need a batting helmet when I play baseball."

Rebecca laughed and picked up the golf ball. They crawled out from under the pines. "Thanks for your help," Rebecca said, brushing the pine needles off her knees.

"My pleasure," said Josh.

She thought he'd start immediately back up the hill, but instead he stood still as if he were waiting for something.

This is your chance! Rebecca told herself. *Say something about how you're looking forward to the trip, how you'll be glad to get to know him better! Don't be shy!* But she couldn't get her mouth to cooperate with her mind.

"Hey, you two!" Kathy yelled. "What's going on there?"

"We found the ball!" Rebecca shouted back. Her heart was heavy with defeat and disappointment, and the rest of the game went by in a blur. Rebecca was only aware of her own silence. The more she thought about it, the more painful it became, and the more obvious, she was sure, it must be to the others.

Meanwhile Kathy sparkled, laughing and joking, completely at ease with both boys. Rebecca was miserable.

As soon as the last hole was played, Rebecca headed for the house. Kathy went with her.

"That was really fun!" she said brightly.

"A blast." Rebecca couldn't quite disguise her sarcasm.

"Hey, don't sound blue. Here comes Prince Charming to give you another chance to be Princess Charming! I've got to run." Kathy gave Rebecca's hand a squeeze. "Talk to you later!"

Eric was still playing golf, but Josh apparently had had enough. Rebecca sat on the stone terrace steps and he joined her.

There was an awkward silence. Rebecca looked down at her blue-jeaned knees and then looked at Josh's knees, which were tanned and bare below his faded Hawaiian shorts.

"I think my mom left some lemonade in the frig," she finally said, poised to jump up and retreat into the house. "Would you like some?"

"No, thanks," said Josh politely. Rebecca settled back on the steps.

Josh tapped his foot on the grass and looked in Eric's direction.

"Your brother and Kathy are quite a pair," he said with a laugh.

"I never really thought of them as a 'pair,'" Rebecca remarked, forcing herself to laugh lightly, too. "But I see what you mean. Lately they've been getting along pretty well. It must be chemistry or something."

Josh smiled and raised an eyebrow. "Chemistry, huh?"

"Well, you know what I mean. Some people just have an affect on certain other people. . . ." Rebecca's voice trailed off weakly.

Josh leaned forward to brush a persistent pine needle from his shin, and as he did his shoulder lightly brushed against hers. A thrill went through Rebecca's body. But once more she was at a loss for words. It seemed that the closer Josh got the shyer she became.

"Yeah, Kathy's a fun girl," Josh said matter-of-factly. "In fact, she reminds me a lot of—someone I used to know in the city."

Suddenly in her mind Rebecca saw two faces side by side, like some kind of slide show. Kathy McBride and Monica DeForest—they *did* look somewhat alike! Rebecca was stunned. The more she thought about it, the more Kathy's latest school picture, which Rebecca carried in her wallet, resembled Monica's most recent *Seventeen* magazine cover. Rebecca felt like a popped balloon.

She looked up from her reverie just in time to catch Josh watching her from the corner of his eye. She suddenly realized that she had never responded to his last comment. Before she could say anything he had looked away and risen to his feet.

"I think there's some yard work waiting for me at home," he explained, too eagerly, Rebecca thought. "Miles of hedges to prune before dark."

"Sure," Rebecca said, standing up. She was very aware of how tall Josh was. Since she kept her eyes on the ground, he was forced to look at the top of her head. He wrinkled his eyebrows. "Did you do something different to your hair?"

Rebecca looked down at one long strand lying on her shoulder. "Actually," she said, embarrassed, "I straightened it a little."

"Hmm," was Josh's only other remark on the subject.

For a long time after Josh left, Rebecca sat on the steps and thought about chemistry. Not the kind of chemistry she had learned in Mr. Blair's class the year before, but the kind of chemistry she was starting to sense happening between Kathy and Eric. The kind of chemistry that clearly *wasn't* happening between her and Josh.

Things hadn't exactly taken off between them. In fact, that day's miniature golf experience made her "lesson" with Josh a couple of weeks before seem like a fireworks display.

And all he had had to say about her new hairstyle was "Hmm."

Basically, Rebecca thought, *all the chemistry's taking place on my side. His effect on me makes up for my lack of effect on him!* She plucked a daisy from the flower border and began tearing off the petals. "He loves me; he loves me not. He loves me; he loves me not. He still loves Monica; he never even met Monica. Kathy reminds him of Monica; Kathy doesn't remind him of Monica at all. He can't wait to go to Canada; he wishes he never said he'd go. He loves me; he loves me not."

Rebecca looked down at the bald stem in her hand and swallowed a lump in her throat. She resolved never to have another crush on a gorgeous, popular first baseman with a taste for models—and never again to straighten her hair.

Chapter Four

Mr. Thompson had rented a van for the four-day drive, and the following Saturday morning at 5:00 A.M. the Thompsons, Josh, and Kathy set out for the Canadian Rockies.

Kathy had slept over at Rebecca's house the night before, and the two girls stayed up talking for hours, so Rebecca understood when she heard Kathy snoring softly fifteen minutes into the trip. Melissa had also fallen asleep, and soon the boys in the back of the van were snoring, too.

Rebecca was left relatively alone with her thoughts and the box of doughnuts her mom passed back to her. She was tired, but not too tired to feel tingly with excitement. Josh was sitting right behind her! She still couldn't believe it. She hoped nothing would happen to spoil what could be the most fun she had ever had in her life. So far, everything was working out pretty well, but then they had only been gone half an hour. All she had to do was keep her cool around Josh—mission impossible! Rebecca sighed at the thought and allowed herself to drift off to sleep.

"Welcome to Canada!" Rebecca woke with a jolt at the sound of Eric's voice. "Where are we?" she mumbled, rubbing her eyes.

"Niagara," said Kathy. She had somehow managed to hook her legs over Rebecca's guitar case, which was on the floor in front of her, and was sipping a can of apple juice.

"About time you woke up, Becky!" Eric leaned his elbows on the back of his seat.

"How long was I asleep?"

"Days," Eric replied. "Wasn't she, Josh?"

Josh looked up from a copy of *Sports Illustrated*. "I wouldn't know," he said with a smile. "I was asleep most of the time myself."

"At least she didn't snore like Kathy did," Eric said teasingly.

Kathy looked shocked. "Is that true, Becky?"

Rebecca laughed. "Just a little bit. So what did I miss while I was asleep?"

"Oh, a big waterfall. Nothing much," Kathy said, restlessly jiggling her foot. She twisted around in her seat. Josh and Eric had just opened their windows so she practically had to shout. "And, I don't remember snoring, Eric! I was too busy dreaming."

"But you were only asleep for half an hour!"

"I still had time for a dream." She glanced at Rebecca. "It was about—the Rockies. Becky and Josh were in it—they were riding double on a beautiful palomino stallion. You, meanwhile . . ."

Rebecca was glad she wasn't behind the wheel—she would have driven off the road. She felt her face turn as red as Kathy's baggy cotton shorts. She turned around quickly and noticed that Josh looked a little uncomfortable, too, although he did smile as Kathy and Eric continued their chatter. Rebecca had no idea what he might be thinking about the idea of riding double with her. She was surprised that Kathy hadn't come right out and asked him!

When Mr. Thompson pulled into a rest area a few minutes later, Rebecca was the first one out of the van. She turned to Kathy in the ladies' room with a look of disbelief. "What was *that* all about? Riding *double* on a palomino *stallion*?" Rebecca pulled a brush from her purse and yanked it through her hair.

"Doesn't that sound romantic?" Kathy leaned over the sink to inspect her reflection and carefully wiped a smudge of mascara from under her eye. "It was the most romantic thing I could think of off the top of my head."

"But why did you have to think of anything at all?" Rebecca twisted her hair into a bun and jabbed it fiercely with a barrette.

"Since you won't say a word to Josh, I thought I'd hint to him that romance might await him where he least expects it. It's not too early in the drive to start planting seeds, you know."

"Yeah, well, seeds are one thing but you might as well have just said that I couldn't wait to have his arms around me, on a horse or anywhere else!" Rebecca looked glum.

"Don't be so paranoid!" Kathy saw Rebecca's expression and relented. "I'm sorry, Becky. I guess I put my foot in my mouth. No more dreams, I promise."

The rest of the day passed quickly and uneventfully. Rebecca half hoped there'd be some seat switching so she could talk to Josh, but everyone kept his place.

At the motel that night the four teenagers did jumping jacks in the parking lot to stretch out while Mr. and Mrs. Thompson picked up room keys in the office.

"What do you say," Eric panted as he jogged in place. "Let's meet later for a secret pizza bash? You two sneak over to our room."

"Great idea!" Josh exclaimed with a glance at Rebecca. She had stopped doing jumping jacks, but her stomach did a few on its own. "Sounds good to me," she said cautiously.

"*Doesn't* sound good to me," said Mr. Thompson firmly as he walked up behind them. "Besides, we only reserved two rooms, so tonight it's going to be dormitory style— women in one, men in the other. You boys'll have to wait till we get to the ranch for your bachelor pad."

"Rats, foiled again!" Eric said, joking.

The group pulled their overnight bags from the van and headed for the rooms. As Rebecca trailed Mrs. Thompson, Melissa, and Kathy through the door, she looked over just in time to catch Josh looking in *her* direction as he trailed Mr. Thompson and Eric. This time he was the one who turned red.

Rebecca felt warm with excitement as she dumped her bag on a bed. She had been surprised by the interesting look in Josh's sea gray eyes. An *interested* look.

She continued to see that look even after she had snuggled into bed and closed her eyes. Josh Kramer had been looking at *her.* Rebecca fell asleep with the feeling that possibly something could happen.

The next day, however, Rebecca realized that absolutely nothing could happen—at least, not in the van. She had thought that spending so much time with Josh in such a small space would force them to talk and get to know each other better. And they actually did sit next to each other a few times, thanks to Kathy's energetic efforts.

But they talked about the weather, and then Josh started a conversation about guitar playing, but because she had forgotten to listen to the albums they had talked about before, Rebecca still felt awkward and out of it. Once when everybody else was napping, she sneaked Eric's baseball cards out of his backpack and studied them so she could talk knowledgeably with Josh about his favorite subject. But she never got further than memorizing the pitching staff for the New York Mets. Not exactly enough to build a relationship on, she thought ruefully. *And face it,* she said to herself, stuffing the cards back where she found them. *Even if I knew the name and vital statistics of every player in the major leagues, I wouldn't know Josh any better.*

The final day of the road trip was clear and sunny. They had turned off all major highways and were traveling on country roads. Kathy and Eric sat side by side in the middle seat, deep in conversation about the prospect of graduating from high school in a year. Josh and Rebecca were in the far back with Melissa, listening to Kathy's portable tape player.

Rebecca was the first to notice a faint black line on the flat horizon. She pointed it out to Josh, who looked up from his tictactoe game with Melissa.

"Is that what I think it is?" she asked, a feeling of awe stealing over her.

"It must be," said Josh in the same tone.

"It's the Rockies!" shouted Eric.

For a long time the black line didn't seem to get any closer. Then suddenly it was as if the mountains rose up all at once right in front of them. Rebecca had never seen anything more beautiful. The pinks and oranges and reds of sunset made it even more spectacular.

Soon they were climbing into the foothills. The van bounced along a steep winding road into the twilight. Up ahead, Rebecca saw the glow of lights in a house, then a sign—the Kicking Horse Ranch! As soon as Mr. Thompson had parked the van, the whole crew tumbled out to take deep breaths of mountain air and enjoy the view, the stars, the dim shadows in the paddock that were horses grazing, a bubbling stream, and the majestic mountains.

Rebecca was aware of Josh standing beside her, his hands pushed deep into the pockets of his jeans. They tipped their heads back and looked up at the same time.

"I've never seen a sky so *big*," she said softly.

"Me, either," he said. "It sure feels like a million miles from New York."

"Doesn't it?" They stood in silence for a moment, and for the first time Rebecca didn't feel self-conscious that she wasn't saying anything witty. She was relaxed and she could feel that Josh was, too. The idea that silence wasn't something to be avoided at all costs took her by surprise.

Just then a tall man in a western-style hat approached the group, a bright stream of light bobbing from his flashlight.

"Evening, folks," he said with a friendly grin. "I'm Clyde Fenster. You must be the Thompsons."

Mr. Thompson shook his hand and made the introductions.

"I see one of you is pretty tuckered out." He nodded at Melissa, asleep in Mrs. Thompson's arms.

"I think we're all exhausted," Rebecca's mother said with a tired smile.

"Then I'll show you right to your quarters."

Everyone grabbed a couple of bags, and they set off across a little bridge. At the top of a small wooded hill there was a clearing dotted with log cabins. Clyde cast the flashlight beam on two slightly larger cabins.

"Those are the bathhouses. There's one for men, one for women." He pulled out two keys. "This one is for Mr. and Mrs. and the little one." He pointed to a cabin and then to its neighbor. "And the girls are over there. The boys'll be on the other side of the hill—I'll show them where. Good night, all. Holler if you need anything!"

The boys disappeared into the dark with Clyde. Rebecca's parents kissed the girls good night and headed for their cabin to tuck Melissa in.

Rebecca and Kathy dropped their bags on the porch of their cabin. "I could sleep right here!" Kathy declared. "Who needs a bed?"

Rebecca couldn't agree more. She twisted the key in the lock and pushed the door open with an effort. Through the darkness she made out a pull chain hanging from the ceiling. When she turned on the light, she instantly loved the room. The twin beds on either side of the cabin were covered with bright white counterpanes, and both the night table and the big, old-fashioned wardrobe were made of warm, worn oak.

Kathy only had eyes for the beds. "I have got to lie down, Becky," she said, "before I absolutely drop!" She belly flopped onto the nearest bed, causing the springs to creak wildly.

Rebecca was already at one of the two big windows peering out at the almost full moon.

"Oh, my gosh!" exclaimed Kathy, suddenly

sitting bolt upright and looking around her in dismay. "Where's the bathroom?"

Rebecca looked around, too. "It must be outside in those bathhouses Clyde was talking about," she said.

"When he said 'bathhouse,' I thought he meant *showers*!" Kathy grimaced. "Are you trying to tell me I have to hike through the bushes where there are probably bears and wolves in the middle of the night just to brush my *teeth*?"

Rebecca laughed.

"Not to mention in the morning," Kathy said, continuing in a despairing tone. "How am I supposed to make it from here to there without anyone seeing me before my make-up's safely in place?"

Rebecca threw a pillow at her.

Kathy jumped up from her bed and stood expectantly by the front door of the cabin. "Well?" she said.

"Well, what?" Rebecca asked.

"Well, aren't you going to come with me to protect me from Bigfoot and whatever else is prowling around out there?"

Rebecca giggled. "Sure. I have to go, too." There was a flashlight on the dresser, and she grabbed it before following Kathy out onto the porch.

Kathy was peering suspiciously into the

darkness. "Do you even remember where the bathhouse is?"

Rebecca gestured vaguely to the left. "It's somewhere over there. I *think.*"

Just then they heard a soft rustling sound from behind a big maple tree not far from the cabin. Rebecca's heart gave a frightened thump. Kathy grabbed her hand.

"Boo!" Eric leapt out from behind the tree. Kathy squealed and Rebecca jumped, dropping the flashlight.

"Did I scare you?" he asked hopefully.

Kathy had recovered and was laughing helplessly. "No, you didn't scare me," she said between giggles. "I always greet my close friends with a scream!"

"Were you going to wait behind that tree all night on the chance that we might come out?" asked Rebecca, retrieving her flashlight.

"Oh, I would have given up after an hour or two." He grinned. "Actually, I think I'm out here for the same reason you are. Need an escort?"

Eric left them in front of the women's bathhouse. Inside they took up posts at adjacent sinks. Kathy looked around the bathhouse critically.

"Well, it could be worse," she admitted, opening her cosmetic case.

"I think it's nice," Rebecca mumbled through

a mouthful of toothpaste. "But then I'm not as picky about my plumbing as you are."

"True, true." Kathy carefully wiped at an eyelid with a cotton ball. She turned to Rebecca with one eye still shadowed in grayish blue and the other bare. "So now that we're here, how do you feel about things with Josh?" she asked seriously.

Rebecca giggled. "I'm sorry, it's just that you look so funny, I don't think I can have a serious conversation with you."

Kathy wiped off her other eye. "There. *Now* can you think straight?"

Rebecca nodded. "So what were you saying?" she asked.

"Josh, Josh, Josh!" Kathy exclaimed. "What do you think?"

"Well—" Rebecca lathered up her washcloth and started scrubbing her face. "You know me. I change my mind every five minutes about how hopeless the situation is."

"That's true," Kathy said. "I've gotten up-to-the-minute reports in gas station restrooms all across the continent!"

The girls had finished washing up and headed back to their cabin. "I'd say it's a question of relative hopelessness," Rebecca said in a whisper in case Eric was still lurking outside. "It's either completely hopeless or not *quite* completely hopeless. Take your pick!"

"I still think you have the wrong perspective on things," Kathy said as they mounted the cabin steps. "You say Josh would never like a girl like you. Maybe that's where you've got it wrong. Maybe you just don't know what kind of girl you *are*. If you ask me, you're the kind of girl a guy like Josh would be lucky to have like him. If you could believe that, then maybe you wouldn't feel so shy."

Kathy had spoken lightly, but her words stayed with Rebecca long after they had climbed into bed and turned off the lights.

Chapter Five

The first rays of sun woke Rebecca. She stretched and yawned, her body stiff from having sat in the van for so long.

Rebecca tossed off her quilt and sat up in bed. Kathy, completely buried under her covers, was snoring lightly. Rebecca knew she should go back to sleep—she hadn't gotten enough rest—but the excitement of finally being at the ranch made it impossible.

Leaning her elbows on the windowsill, she gazed out at the morning. A haze was just lifting in the distance, revealing a breathtaking view of jagged, dark, snow-covered mountains. Rebecca had never seen anything so wild and beautiful. It was like a *National Geographic* cover, in real life.

"Becky, could you pull down the shade? Please?" Rebecca turned around to catch her friend's sleepy face peeking out from beneath the covers.

"Good morning!" Rebecca said cheerfully.

Kathy pulled a pillow over her head. "It's still the middle of the night as far as I'm concerned."

"But the sun's up," Rebecca said, pointing outside.

"Where? I don't see it!" Kathy's voice was muffled. "It still looks pretty dark to me."

"Well, I'm ready to rise and shine," Rebecca said.

"You go ahead and do that. I'll just sleep a little longer."

Rebecca grabbed some clothes and a towel, picked up her old riding boots, and tiptoed out the door.

The morning was perfectly still. In the daylight the cabins looked even more rustic. The pines and hardwood trees had taken on a brilliant green. Rebecca took a deep breath of cool, fragrant air and sat down on the stairs to pull on her boots. She giggled—they looked great with her nightgown. Well, she was pretty sure she was the only person awake in the camp. She put on her denim jacket and started across the clearing toward the bathhouse.

Josh was coming down the path from the opposite direction, his blond hair wet from a shower. Rebecca just about ran into him.

"Whoops!" she exclaimed. "I wasn't looking where I was going. I didn't expect anybody else to be up!"

"I can see that," Josh said, smiling at her outfit.

Rebecca blushed and laughed at the same time. She was always shy about her appearance and was a conservative dresser, to say the least. It was basically a nightmare to be caught by Josh Kramer in her nightgown. But it was also incredibly funny.

"I'm on my way to the shower," she explained, clutching her clothes to her chest.

"I didn't think you were on your way to the stables," said Josh. They both laughed again.

"Well, see you." Rebecca started toward the bathhouse again, eager to escape.

"Hey—" Josh stopped her with a hand on her arm. Rebecca froze. Suddenly she was aware of how gorgeous he looked that morning with his hair slicked back. A faded black T-shirt made his gray eyes seem deeper. She felt goose bumps rise on her arm under his hand.

"Were you going to have breakfast?" he asked.

"Breakfast?" Rebecca sounded as though she had never heard of such a thing.

"Why don't we walk over together, after your shower?"

"I'd like that," Rebecca said, avoiding his eyes.

"Then I'll meet you back here in about fifteen minutes. That enough time for you?"

"Plenty." Rebecca smiled to assure him.

Josh smiled, too, and turned on his heel to leave. Rebecca remained planted in the path, staring at his retreating back, then scurried into the bathhouse. She could hardly stand still long enough to shampoo and condition her hair. She was having breakfast with Josh!

After her shower she dressed quickly and then studied herself in the mirror. She hadn't brought any makeup from her cabin. She'd have to do without.

Her hair, on the other hand—*blecch*! Rebecca thought, sticking out her tongue at her reflection. No time to blow it dry, and if she left it down it would just go wild. She decided on a tight french braid—not glamorous, maybe, but at least controlled.

Exactly fifteen minutes after she had parted from Josh, Rebecca peeked out the bathhouse door. Her heart sank—there was no sign of Josh. Maybe he had decided to have breakfast with someone else. She probably shouldn't be surprised.

"Hey!"

Rebecca jumped as Josh emerged from some trees near the men's bathhouse. She waved, relieved.

Josh smiled at her as she joined him on the path. "Let's go," he said. "I'm starved!"

They fell into step, side by side, following green wooden signs that said Cook House. Pretty soon they didn't need the signs—the delicious smell of bacon frying and bread toasting led them.

Rebecca's eyes strayed to the sky and back to the path. Josh was so close to her that she couldn't bring herself to look at him.

They reached the bridge they had crossed the night before. In the daylight it was beautiful—old, wooden, and just rickety enough to be charming without being dangerous. Beyond it a meadow sloped up to a rambling white house with green shutters. Next to the house were a couple of red, barnlike buildings, one was the cook house.

As they walked by the house, a white-haired woman in a flowered dress called to them from the porch. "Good morning! Heading for the cook house?"

"Yes!" Josh called back as Rebecca waved a greeting.

"Stop by after you've eaten!" The woman nodded them on with a smile.

"I wonder who she is?" Rebecca whispered.

"Maybe the owner of the ranch," Josh said.

Inside the cook house four men in jeans and work shirts were eating at a long table. Behind a counter on the left an older man with gray-streaked red hair, wearing a white apron and chef's hat, flipped pancakes on the grill of a wood-burning stove.

"That looks great," Josh said. He rubbed his stomach. "I feel hungry enough to eat a bear."

Rebecca felt as if she had so many butterflies in her stomach that there wouldn't be room for anything else.

They stepped up to the counter and ordered pancakes and bacon. Bob, the cook, threw some bacon onto the grill. As they stood watching it sizzle, a tall man in a brown cowboy hat stepped into the line behind them. "Morning, folks," he said, tipping his hat to Rebecca.

"Hi," Rebecca said politely. Josh echoed her.

The man looked them up and down in a friendly way, his gaze resting on Josh's worn-out hiking boots. "You come to break some ponies, son?" he asked, speaking with a slight French-Canadian accent.

"No." Josh smiled broadly. "To tell you the truth I don't even know how to ride, but I'm hoping to learn."

The man laughed. "I'm Guy," he said, extending his hand.

"Nice to meet you." Josh took his hand firmly. "I'm Josh, and this is Rebecca."

"Nice to meet you," Rebecca said, smiling shyly when Guy winked at her.

Bob handed them their breakfast trays, and

Rebecca and Josh sat down at one of the long empty tables. Rebecca watched as Josh happily poured about half a pitcher of golden brown syrup over his pancakes. Suddenly her own appetite returned full force. She dug into her breakfast with relish.

She and Josh ate in a silence that was punctuated, for the most part, only by an occasional smile or laugh.

They had just finished their breakfast, and Rebecca was starting to worry about what to say to Josh when her family and Kathy walked into the dining hall with Clyde Fenster.

Kathy, dressed in white jeans and a powder blue T-shirt, smiled at them as she joined the line at the grill. Eric approached Josh and Rebecca, still rubbing sleep out of his eyes.

"How can you be yawning?" Josh asked, kidding him. "*Some* of us have been up for hours!"

"Really?" Eric said. Rebecca hoped Josh didn't pick up on the undercurrent in Eric's bland comment. She couldn't miss it, especially since Eric wiggled his eyebrows at her when Josh wasn't looking.

She frowned at him, but he had already turned to join the others. It reminded her that she had never confronted her brother to ask him how much he knew about her crush.

She finished her second orange juice quickly,

now feeling uncomfortable sitting there with Josh. She was relieved when the rest of her family sat with them, and she thought Josh looked relieved, too. His eyes lit up as he asked Kathy how she had liked her first night "roughing it."

Rebecca felt a sudden pang. A few minutes earlier all Josh's animation had been directed toward his pancakes; now he was talking up a storm. Had he been nervous sitting alone with her, or just bored? She didn't like the way he looked at Kathy, or the way Kathy laughed at his question, even though she always laughed that way.

"I hear you had an encounter with a wild animal last night," Josh was saying.

Kathy laughed again. "That's right!" she said, darting a playful look at Eric. "Wild's the word for this species. It had brown hair and walked on its hind legs. Pretty scary!"

Josh's gray eyes crinkled at the corners, making him look extra adorable to Rebecca. She became instantly jealous that his smile wasn't aimed at her. *Don't be ridiculous*, she chastised herself firmly. *Just because I had Josh alone for a few minutes doesn't mean anything. Just because he came on vacation with my family doesn't mean anything. At least*, she thought, looking from Josh to Kathy, *I don't think it does.*

"Are you kids interested in stopping by the

Valoises' house after breakfast?" asked Mrs. Thompson. Everyone had finished eating but Melissa, who was still attacking a stack of flapjacks almost as tall as she was.

"They're the people who own the Kicking Horse, right?" Eric asked.

His mother nodded as she wiped some syrup from Melissa's cheek with a paper napkin.

"I think we saw Mrs. Valois on our way here this morning." Josh looked to Rebecca for confirmation.

"Yeah, and she did say to drop in," she agreed.

"Well, let's go!" Mr. Thompson pushed his chair back and stood up. "That is, unless anyone wants to finish Melissa's breakfast." Melissa giggled with delight as her father picked her up and swung her in the air.

Clyde Fenster joined them as they walked over to the white house. He introduced them to Pierre and Marie Valois, who were very friendly and welcoming. Mrs. Valois gave them a quick tour of the house. "You should think of this house as your temporary home," she said, smiling at each of them in turn. "I love company, and I hope you'll stop in often!"

"It's a beautiful house," Mrs. Thompson said sincerely. "Do you live here in the winter, too?"

Mrs. Valois nodded. "Year-round. We love it too much to leave it even for a few months.

Of course, the cabins are only rented during the summer season. You're the only ones here this week, but we expect large groups for the rest of the summer."

Out on the porch again, Clyde looked at Rebecca, Kathy, Josh, and Eric and raised his bushy eyebrows. "What do you say we check out the stables?"

They were all enthusiastic. Rebecca was both excited and nervous—it was a long time since she had been on a horse! As they passed the bunkhouse and approached the barn, she sniffed the sweet smell of hay and horses and her excitement grew.

The group walked through an open doorway that was wide enough and tall enough for a horse and rider to pass through. Inside, the earth floor was covered with hay. On either side of the central aisle were rows of stalls, and Rebecca could see a few horses peeking out.

Clyde made a clucking sound with his tongue, and a few more heads poked out. "Horses are just like people," he said. "Take Clown here." He grabbed the brown, whiskery muzzle of one of the horses and gave it a gentle shake. Clown stood passively, his ears pointed forward and his dark eyes glued attentively to Clyde, clearly enjoying the attention.

"Clown's a people horse," Clyde said. "He'll

talk to anyone. Then you've got Hickory—he can do without company." The four peered over Clyde's shoulder into the stall next to Clown's. All they could see were a large gray rump and a long tail swishing at flies. Hickory munched his breakfast without turning in their direction.

Josh, Eric, and Kathy followed Clyde farther down the left side of the barn as he continued to point out and name the horses. But Rebecca was diverted by a friendly chestnut across the aisle from Hickory. When she approached its stall, the horse lifted its lip over its teeth in what looked like a smile. Rebecca smiled back and held out her hand. The horse moved its muzzle near her hand, snorted noisily, and nudged her. Rebecca knew she had been checked out and accepted. Now she stroked the chestnut's neck gently but firmly. "Hey, there," she said in a low voice.

"Someone likes you," Clyde said as he moved back to join Rebecca. "This is Gingernut. She looks like a softie, but believe it or not she's the leader of the herd. Want to try her?"

Rebecca nodded eagerly. "I'd love to!"

"Good. I'll get you on her as soon as we pick out horses for everybody else."

Rebecca felt Josh's eyes on her as she stood by Gingernut's stall. When she turned her head, she caught him staring. He looked away immediately, appearing to study a halter hanging on a hook outside one of the stalls. Rebecca felt her cheek grow pink as she laid it against the horse's warm neck. If she didn't know better she'd have thought she saw admiration in Josh's eyes. But she knew better. He was probably looking at Gingernut!

Clyde was lecturing again. "This is Guy," he said. "He's your main man when it comes to horses. He'll teach you how to saddle and groom." He gestured at the tall cowboy who had just entered the barn and was strolling up to greet them.

Guy took a pair of worn leather chaps from a closet cluttered with saddles, bridles, and other riding equipment, and as he buckled them over his jeans, he and Clyde discussed which mounts would be best for which riders.

"Judging from what I've seen around the barn just now, we've got one experienced rider and three beginners," Clyde said.

Josh and Eric grinned sheepishly. "We're that easy to peg, huh?" said Josh. Kathy, who had been looking apprehensive, jumped just then as Clown nudged her from behind. "I'm a beginner!" she yelped hastily.

Meanwhile, Rebecca felt a small glow of pride. Clyde thought she looked like an experienced rider—more experienced than the others. She could do something they couldn't. She bubbled with enthusiasm as she helped Clyde and Guy lead four horses from their stalls into the center aisle. First Gingernut and Clown and then two pintos that Guy introduced as Mac and Joan of Arc. He hooked the horses' halters to lead ropes dangling from the rafter above the aisle, then he pulled a bucketful of combs, hoof picks, and curry brushes from the closet.

"Okay, everyone grab a brush and a horse!" While Guy demonstrated, the four began grooming their mounts. Eric took Clown. "How appropriate!" Kathy said. Josh worked energetically on Joan of Arc's coat. Kathy dabbed gingerly at Mac with an oval curry brush.

Rebecca put her all into grooming Gingernut. She faced the mare's hind end, so she wouldn't be surprised by a kick. Everything she had learned when she was younger came back to her.

Kathy glanced down at her spotless white jeans with regret. Guy caught her look. "We can take care of that," he said with a smile. He disappeared into the barn and returned with a pair of chaps, like his but smaller. "Try these!"

Kathy fumbled with the buckles and zippers and then straightened up. She turned in a circle and giggled. "How do I look, guys?"

Eric whistled. "You're definitely going to start a fashion trend."

"That's for sure," Josh said. "But can you ride?"

They all mounted and started off on a trail ride with Guy in the lead on Hickory and Rebecca and Gingernut bringing up the rear. By then the sun had gotten high enough to warm the air, and it was a beautiful morning. The trail was dappled with leafy sun and shade patterns, and the scent of pine and wildflowers was everywhere.

"You ride pretty well," Josh told Rebecca, falling in beside her. He smiled down at her, the breeze lifting the blond hair off his forehead.

"You're not so bad yourself," she said shyly.

They rode to the edge of a meadow in silence, both facing forward and focusing on Eric and Kathy's backs. The two in front appeared to be carrying on an entertaining conversation, their heads frequently were turned to each other. At one point Eric threw his head back and laughed uproariously; at another he reached over to tickle Kathy, and his lurching sent Clown into a trot, which caused Mac to also break into a trot and both riders were nearly thrown.

They started on a narrower trail leading into the woods and had to go single file. Rebecca found herself riding in front of Josh and behind Kathy. She watched Kathy's long blond hair swing in the wind, conscious of her own thick french braid, which was definitely not swinging. Josh couldn't help but compare the two of them from his vantage point, and Rebecca was sure she knew which of them would make the more favorable impression.

Humph! she thought, squeezing Gingernut's sides with her heels. Suddenly she just wanted to get away from the others. She trotted Gingernut to the front of the line.

"Guy, can I canter her for a little way?" she asked.

"Sure, go ahead. Don't let her get away from you, though. She's kind of frisky."

"I won't go far," Rebecca said, reassuring him. "We'll turn back in a few minutes."

Rebecca urged Gingernut into a canter, using her reins and legs the way she had been taught. She had been so eager to start moving that she and Gingernut were flying before Rebecca remembered that she hadn't ridden in a long time and she should be a little scared to go so fast.

But then, she thought, there was really nothing to be frightened of. She was riding! Gingernut's pace was smooth and rhythmic. Rebecca simply relaxed in the saddle and her ride was almost as comfortable as sitting on a sofa.

After a short distance, she slowed Gingernut to a trot. Aside from the mare's hoofbeats and the singing of the birds there wasn't a sound. She felt alone in the world.

It was such a perfect moment that Rebecca wanted it to last forever, but she knew she shouldn't stray too far on her own. She cantered back the way they had come. She reached what she thought was the spot where she had left the others, but there was no one in sight. For a second her heart contracted and her palms grew damp. For all the beauty of the morning she suddenly realized how awful it would be to get lost there. The ranch was in wild country—in some directions a person could ride for a day and never come across another house or farm.

Just as Rebecca was starting to panic she entered the meadow they had passed through earlier. There were Guy, Josh, Eric, and Kathy, the latter three trotting in a big circle around the cowboy, who was shouting instructions.

"Chin up, Kathy! Looks good, Josh. Sit back in the saddle and roll with the horse, Eric, then you won't bounce."

Rebecca waved, weak with relief. Guy caught sight of her and touched the brim of his hat. "Just waiting for you, Becky, and trying to teach them something while we're at it. Let's head back, folks!"

Kathy pulled Mac to a halt. "Hey, Becky! This isn't as hard as I thought it would be!"

Rebecca grinned. "I'm glad you like it! You'll

be ready for a rodeo before you know it." Her grin faded slightly when Josh joined Kathy as they left the meadow, leaving Eric riding next to Rebecca. *It doesn't mean anything,* she said to herself. *They have a lot to talk about—it's the first time either of them has gone horseback riding, that's all.*

She tried not to let her feelings show, and she must have succeeded because Eric didn't ask any questions. Instead he raved about the ride.

"Yeah, this is a lot more fun than I expected!" He patted Clown's neck enthusiastically. "Maybe I'll stay out here after y'all go home and be a cowpoke for the rest of the summer." He twirled an imaginary lasso.

"Great idea," Rebecca said. "More room in the van on the way home for the rest of us!"

"Oh, I don't know." Eric looked at her slyly. "I kind of got the feeling you didn't mind the close quarters."

Rebecca blushed. "I don't know what you mean."

Eric shrugged and started whistling "Home on the Range." Rebecca looked for a way to change the subject. She focused on Josh and Kathy again and then turned back to her brother. "It's a good thing Josh and Kathy get along so well," she observed casually. "Did you, uh, by any chance mention that Kathy would probably be coming when you invited Josh?"

Rebecca was sure the question came out incredibly obvious and awkward, but Eric didn't blink. "I don't know. I probably did," he said, dropping his feet from the stirrups and swinging them. "He was pretty psyched, as I recall. Said he didn't know either of you too well, but he'd like to." He grinned. "I assured him you weren't worth the trouble."

"Thanks for nothing!" Rebecca passed the conversation off lightly, but inside she felt just a little bit sick. She didn't have proof that Josh was interested in Kathy any more than she had proof that the picture in his locker was of Monica DeForest, but it wasn't impossible. That was enough to add a chill to an otherwise flawless summer day.

Chapter Six

There were so many things to do on the ranch that the first day flew by. Rebecca got the feeling the whole vacation might be that way. What if it ended and she and Josh weren't any closer than they were right then?

The two girls were changing into bathing suits and putting extra clothes in backpacks before heading to Green Lake for a sunset swim and cookout that evening.

"So what do you think about the ranch as a place to fall in love?" asked Kathy as she adjusted the straps on her bright pink- and white-flowered bikini. "It looks to me like you and Josh are on your way!"

Rebecca pulled a T-shirt over her green one-piece suit. She snorted. "You've got to be kidding!"

"On the contrary." Kathy slipped her feet

into a pair of sandals. "He seemed pretty impressed with your riding."

"No more than he was with yours," Rebecca said.

Kathy didn't pick up on the insinuation. "Yep, he was very impressed," she said. "Especially when you took Gingernut over those jumps Guy set up for you after the ride. You were fantastic. You should have seen his face!"

"It really wasn't anything." Rebecca pushed the door open and they left the cabin.

"Don't be so modest!" exclaimed Kathy.

They trudged down a path that ran parallel to the stream, following signs to the lake. "I just don't like being the center of attention, that's all," Rebecca said.

"Why not?" Kathy was curious. "Isn't it fun?"

"I guess." Rebecca hesitated. "But—"

"No 'buts' about it!" The trees were thinning and they could see the lake ahead. "Everyone deserves a turn in the spotlight. Josh has the baseball field—now you have a chance to shine a little."

Rebecca looked at her friend, confused. "How does that fit in with your theory about playing up to a guy's interests and stuff?"

"That's still a good thing to do, don't get me wrong!" Kathy said. "Guys definitely love it. But they also like a girl who can hold her own, who's interesting in her own way."

Rebecca shook her head. "How do you know all this?"

Kathy laughed. "It's the Kathy McBride method, tried and true."

Mr. and Mrs. Thompson, Melissa, and the boys were already settled on the shore of Green Lake. The surrounding trees and mountains were mirrored on the crystal surface of the lake. The Valoises were also there with Clyde, who was building a fire in an open barbecue pit.

Rebecca and Kathy joined Eric and Josh at the edge of the water. "What do you say? Last one in buys pizza for everyone back at our cabins tonight?" Josh said with a grin.

"You find a pizza parlor in this neighborhood and you're on!" Kathy joked back.

The two girls splashed into the lake, arms waving. Rebecca was glad to go in so she wouldn't have to stand beside Josh feeling shy in her bathing suit. The water was cold, but refreshing. When it hit her thighs, Rebecca dove in. She came up laughing, ready to shout to the boys, but they were already in and making even more noise than she and Kathy had.

They swam past her, racing. She and Kathy climbed onto a rock a few feet from the shore and sat with their feet dangling over the edge. Rebecca shook the water from her hair. She could hear Eric and Josh teasing each other as they ducked in and out of the water.

Then she felt a flick of water on her back. Josh had his hands on the rock. "Come back in, you two!"

Kathy glanced at Rebecca significantly. "No thanks," she said cheerfully. "But you go ahead, Becky."

Rebecca hoped Josh didn't see the shove Kathy gave her. She slipped off the rock and into the water. That time it didn't seem so cold, just cold enough to make her body tingle pleasantly. Her long braid lay down the center of her back as she swam beside Josh. He smiled at her and she smiled back.

Suddenly she felt a tug on her foot. Visions of the Loch Ness monster flashed through her head. "Help!" she hollered as she felt another tug. This one took her halfway under.

She came back up sputtering to see Eric also emerge. "Gotcha!" he gasped.

"Oh, you!" she exclaimed. She paddled angrily toward the shore, trying to catch her breath. Josh swam a smooth crawl beside her. When they got close enough to touch the lake bottom with their feet, he put a hand on her back.

"I was ready to rescue you back there," he said gallantly. "I thought you were going under for good!"

Rebecca got goose bumps, and not from the cold water. "I'm all right," she said, her teeth chattering. She was a little embarrassed that she had made such a fuss over her brother's prank, but she didn't mind Josh's hand on her back at all.

She looked over her shoulder as she stepped from the water. Eric had joined Kathy on the rock—they were sitting close together silhouetted against the low, late-afternoon sun.

Rebecca and Josh stopped on the shore and turned to face each other. He still had his hand on her back, but now he dropped it.

"Uh—would you like something to drink?" he asked.

"I'm not really thirsty," she said. "I've swallowed half the lake already!"

Josh laughed. "Well, I could use a Coke. And you could probably use a seat by the campfire to warm up." He led her to where the others were sitting and, grabbing a towel, put it around her shoulders. That gesture warmed Rebecca more than any campfire could.

Rebecca stood as close to the fire as she dared, hoping her bathing suit would dry fast so she could retreat into the comfortable bulkiness of her jeans and a sweatshirt. The sun had had begun to set, and she could feel the warmth of the day being replaced by cool night air.

By the time Kathy and Eric came in from their swim, the ribs on the barbecue were ready. Rebecca sat next to Josh and across from Kathy and Eric at the picnic table.

She glanced at her brother and Kathy. It was dark now, and in the firelight their eyes glowed with laughter and excitement. She knew hers were glowing, too. If sitting next to Josh in a crowded van had been a thrill, sitting next to him at the picnic table on a magical evening was indescribable.

When all the plates were empty and everyone was full, Clyde added wood to the fire and the group moved to sit around it. They roasted marshmallows that no one had room to eat. Guy got out a harmonica and another ranch hand produced a guitar, and the two started singing cowboy songs.

Rebecca and Josh were sitting side by side on a log, slightly apart from the others. Rebecca felt tense with expectation.

"Why don't you take a turn on the guitar?" Josh asked softly.

Rebecca was surprised and pleased and scared all at the same time. She looked at the other faces around the fire and shook her head emphatically.

"I couldn't," she said with a timid smile. Something in Josh's face made her continue. "I'd like to, but I'm too—shy. I mean, in front of so many people." She was astonished at herself for making such a confession to Josh when she wanted him to think she was poised and confident.

But Josh didn't laugh or say she was silly.

He smiled at her. "I know where you're coming from," he said, his voice low. "I'd feel exactly the same way. I just thought I'd ask because I'd really like to hear you play. I figured you might be braver than I'd be in the same situation."

Rebecca's green eyes widened in disbelief. She pointed to herself. *"Me?"*

"Sure. You!"

Rebecca shook her head again. "You must have the wrong Becky Thompson," she said. "This one's hardly what I'd call 'brave.' "

Josh intently studied the toes of his tennis shoes. The firelight flickered on his downcast face and his bright blond hair. Suddenly Rebecca thought, *Hey, he's shy, too.*

He turned to her, his eyes thoughtful. "No, I don't think I have the wrong person in mind," he said simply. "And it's *Rebecca* Thompson I was talking about." He grinned. "She's always seemed to me like the kind of girl who has the world where she wants it. She's different, she does her own thing. I think that's pretty cool."

Rebecca felt light-headed. She didn't know what to say. She tightly gripped the log they were sitting on, feeling the rough bark dig into her hands. Was it really Josh Kramer saying those things to her? *The* Josh Kramer? She couldn't understand how he could think she was interesting at all.

She expressed her doubts out loud. "It's really not that way for me," she said, her voice barely audible.

Josh reached for a dark blue sweater lying on the ground and pulled it on over his wrinkled white oxford cloth shirt. "Believe it or not, I used to feel about baseball the way you feel about your guitar right now. Freshman year at my old school I didn't even try out for the team even though inside I thought I was good enough to make it. I was chicken! So I spent the spring watching from the stands, but by the end of the season I knew I had to go for it the next year. And I did."

Rebecca was amazed at this speech. She realized suddenly that she was staring at Josh with her mouth open, so she closed it with a pop. She felt a flush of warmth. Josh was confiding in her. He must trust her—he must *like* her.

Josh looked toward the others. Rebecca followed his gaze and saw Eric gesturing to them. He was holding a dozing Melissa in his arms, and Kathy was standing next to him.

"Hey, guys!" he called out. "Kathy and Melissa are tired, so I'm going to walk them back to the cabins." In the firelight Rebecca could see her brother grin. "Becky, I thought you said Kathy was going to be *fun*. We should have brought a baby-sitter for her!" Kathy yawned sheepishly and waved goodbye.

Most of the ranch hands had already left. Mr. and Mrs. Thompson were standing by the lake looking out over the moonlit water with their arms around each other.

Rebecca looked back at Josh. Somehow the mood he'd been in seemed to have snapped. "Well, that's the story of my baseball career," he said lightly. "Real inspirational, huh? Actually, it was my—a friend of mine who helped talk me into trying out. Another person's encouragement can really make a difference."

Josh stood up matter-of-factly and Rebecca followed suit. She felt a pang of disappointment. So Josh was talking to her like a little sister—just what she needed! Not only that but he had clearly made a reference to Monica DeForest, one which made it only too plain how different she must be from Rebecca.

She must have sighed more loudly than she had intended because Josh looked at her with concern. "You must be sleepy, too. Want me to walk you back? I've got a flashlight."

Rebecca fumbled in her backpack. "Kathy must have our flashlight." She looked apologetic. "Do you mind?"

"Of course not!"

There wasn't a light on in the girls' cabin when Rebecca and Josh reached the clearing. "I guess she's in bed already," Rebecca whispered. "I'll see you tomorrow."

"Wait a minute," said Josh, putting a firm

hand on her arm. "Will you look at that moon?" He pointed to the wide open sky above them.

Rebecca looked up. The moon was so pale and pure and beautiful that it took her breath away. They stood together for a long moment, then Josh turned toward her. Rebecca could feel his eyes on her face, and a chill ran down her spine. When she turned and met his gaze, she knew he was going to kiss her.

Josh put his hands gently on her shoulders and leaned down. Rebecca closed her eyes. His lips brushed her cheek and then found her mouth and lingered there. The kiss was warm and sweet and firm, and while it lasted Rebecca was sure there was no one and nothing else in the world but her and the moon and Josh.

When they broke apart, Rebecca felt awkward again. She felt her cheeks grow hot.

"Good night," Josh said softly. He kissed her lightly on the forehead and turned to go.

After he had disappeared into the darkness, Rebecca managed to move her feet again. She climbed the steps to the cabin, her mind whirling. She opened the door as quietly as she could and then jumped when she heard Kathy's voice.

"Did he kiss you?" her friend asked excitedly.

In the moonlight coming through the window, Rebecca could just make out Kathy sitting on the side of her bed.

"I heard you two coming," she said apologetically. "I peeked, but just for a minute."

"Yeah, he kissed me," Rebecca said, dazed.

Kathy sighed. "It's so romantic, Becky. And it's only the first day here!"

"I can't believe it," Rebecca admitted softly. "It was too good to be true." She sat on her bed and leaned over the night table to take out her contacts and put them in their case. She began to unbraid her hair slowly.

Kathy burrowed back under her covers. "Well, good night, Beck. I'm still half-asleep, so we'll have to go over the details in the morning. I guess I don't need to tell you to have sweet dreams!"

"No, not tonight." Rebecca pulled her legs into bed and tugged the blanket up to her chin. She smiled to herself in the dark. She had kissed Josh!

She fell asleep still smiling.

Chapter Seven

The second morning at the ranch dawned as sunny and fresh as the first. That day Kathy managed to get up at the same time as Rebecca. "So, how does it feel to be in love?" Kathy asked, yawning.

"I'm not sure," Rebecca answered honestly, thumbing through the T-shirts in her drawer.

"Wear the apricot-colored one," said Kathy. "It complements your complexion."

Rebecca pulled the T-shirt on and tucked it into her jeans. She looked at herself in the mirror and frowned. "Not a very exciting outfit."

Kathy joined her. "Maybe a belt?" she said helpfully. She looked from Rebecca's clothes to her face. "Wow, Becky, you look worn out!"

"I don't think I slept a wink last night,"

Rebecca said sheepishly. "Or the night before, come to think of it."

Kathy grinned. "Too excited, huh? I sure can't blame you!"

Rebecca felt a funny growling in her stomach. "After everything I ate last night at the barbecue I have no right to be hungry, but my stomach seems to have a mind of its own!"

"Mine, too," said Kathy. She peered at Rebecca's face knowingly. "But I bet you're not so much hungry as a victim of the morning-after-the-first-kiss butterflies. Am I right?"

Rebecca patted her stomach uncertainly. "I guess so," she said. "I guess I'm nervous about seeing Josh."

"Well, don't sweat it," Kathy said cheerfully, smoothing her honey blond hair back into a slightly off-center ponytail. "After last night, the rest should be a breeze!"

They started off for the cook house. The grass was still dewy, and after a few steps their sneakers were soaked. *The rest should be a breeze*," Rebecca repeated silently to herself. *"Don't sweat it."* She tried to match the bounce in Kathy's carefree step and failed. *If it should be breeze, then why am I in a panic?*

She knew as soon as she walked into the cook house and saw Josh in the breakfast line that no matter what had happened the night before, one thing hadn't changed. He was still glamorous, popular Josh Kramer, and she was still Rebecca Thompson, not the kind of girl he'd go out with, not the kind of girl he could really like.

It was a painful thought, but it didn't prevent her from flushing with pleasure when she and Kathy joined the line and he flashed her a smile.

"Morning," he said.

Rebecca's mouth went dry. "Hi, Josh," she said, barely managing to answer.

Kathy was only having juice and a muffin, and Bob handed it to her at the same time Josh's breakfast was ready. The two took their trays to the table where Mr. and Mrs. Thompson and Melissa were sitting. Rebecca was left standing in line with Eric.

"So how long did you and Josh stay by the campfire?" Eric asked innocently.

"Oh, not much after you left," she said as casually as she could.

"Come to think of it, I guess I did hear Josh come in," Eric said. He raised one eyebrow. "Come to *think* of it, I guess I remember Josh saying he enjoyed walking you home." He winked broadly. "If you know what I mean!"

Rebecca blushed. "You're awful!" she said in a whisper. "You've got the completely wrong idea."

"It's hard not to," Eric whispered back.

Rebecca picked up her eggs and bacon and turned her back on her twin indignantly.

At the breakfast table Mr. and Mrs. Thompson did most of the talking. Rebecca was secretly relieved. Looking back and forth from her mother to her father while they chattered gave her an excuse to avoid meeting Josh's eyes.

"Yes, I'm feeling nice and relaxed," Mr. Thompson said, biting into a blueberry muffin with a satisfied expression.

"That's what vacations are for," Mrs. Thompson said. "I just hope going to Calgary today for the first session of the conference doesn't spoil your mood!"

"Nothing could," he assured her. "What are you folks going to do to keep busy?"

"Well, Melissa and I are going for a row on Green Lake." Mrs. Thompson turned to the little girl and gave her a smile. "I can't answer for the big kids, though."

"We have riding lessons," said Kathy. "Guy wants to make sure we're all comfortable on horseback before we go on the overnight pack trip."

Only when everyone got up to bus their trays did Rebecca realize she hadn't touched her breakfast. She had been too busy pretending to listen to her parents and looking at Josh out of the corner of her eye.

Josh caught Rebecca going out the door. It

wasn't hard to do because she had stopped to tie her shoe.

"When's your lesson with Guy?" he asked leaning one arm against the wall.

"This afternoon," Rebecca said, looking up from the very careful knot she was working on. When she stood up again, she knew her face was pink to the tips of her ears. She wanted to say something to prolong their conversation, but she was tongue-tied.

Luckily Josh wanted to say something, too. "I was thinking," he said, "maybe after my lesson this morning, we could go for a walk or something. Eric and I discovered a really neat spot yesterday—a beaver dam—it's not far away. . . ." His voice trailed off and he looked at her expectantly.

Rebecca couldn't help smiling. "A beaver dam?"

Josh laughed and shrugged. "Yep. Want to check it out?"

"Sure!"

Josh touched her arm lightly as he turned to head for the stables. "I'll come by your cabin after I ride."

Rebecca caught up with Kathy on the path back to their cabin. She knew her eyes were sparkling.

"What happened back there?" Kathy asked eagerly. "I've been dying of curiosity!"

"I'm going on a date!" Rebecca was breath

less. She crossed her arms across her chest and squeezed herself.

"What!" Kathy stopped in her tracks.

"He asked me on a date—to a beaver pond!"

"A beaver pond?" Kathy exclaimed.

"Where else is there to go on a ranch?" Rebecca said with a giggle.

"Well, that's great!" Kathy gave Rebecca a quick warm hug.

"Yeah, it is," Rebecca said. "But—" She paused.

Kathy read the doubt in Rebecca's eyes. "But what?" she asked kindly.

The girls reached their cabin and sat down on the porch steps. "To tell you the truth, I'm scared," Rebecca said.

"Becky, you're nuts!" Kathy shook her head, mystified. "Scared of what?"

"Scared that I'll blow it." Rebecca sighed. "Scared that there's not anything to blow."

"Hold it right there, Rebecca Thompson," Kathy said. "Inside, on the double. We're going to talk."

Kathy swung open the door, marched Rebecca inside, and sat her down on her bed.

"Now, just what do you mean by 'blowing it'?" Kathy asked, staring her friend squarely in the face. "What's the worst that could happen?"

Rebecca put her feet on the bed and pulled her knees up to her chin. "The worst thing that could happen is my contact would fall out again and I'd look like an idiot and Josh would end up hating me."

"Let's not even consider that," Kathy said impatiently. "What's the second worst thing that could happen?"

"Well, I could get tongue-tied, which happens in about seventy-five percent of my conversations with him," Rebecca said. "Kathy, you just don't know how that feels. It's a nightmare."

"I don't understand why you're so shy, Becky," Kathy said. "Your brother certainly isn't."

"That's just it!" Rebecca grabbed a pillow and gave it a punch. "It's always been that way. Eric's funny and outgoing and I'm—*boring*."

Kathy groaned. "You are *not* boring, Becky! And Josh doesn't think so, either. Good grief— didn't he kiss you last night?"

"That's just it," Rebecca said helplessly. "Last night was amazing. I *felt* amazing. But then this morning I started worrying about whether Josh really liked me or whether for him it was just a kiss—"

"Oh, brother!" Kathy exclaimed, throwing up her hands.

"And I don't know how I'm supposed to *act*—"

Kathy snorted. "Becky, you're talking like you've never even kissed a boy before."

Rebecca was indignant. "Of course I've kissed *boys* before!" Kathy raised one eyebrow and Rebecca shrugged. "Okay, maybe I've only kissed a couple—I'm not an expert like you. But this is different."

"In what way?" Kathy leaned her elbows on her knees with her chin in her hands.

"It's different because I like Josh so much more than I've ever liked any guy before. And he's different because he's, well, he's Josh Kramer!" Rebecca closed her eyes tightly for a moment, struggling to make sense out of her confused feelings. "Josh is just so *special*. Any girl would be so lucky if he liked her. Half—all!—the girls at Hudson Falls High would kill to go out with him."

Kathy cut her off with a wave. "Wait a minute. Josh might be special but that doesn't have anything to do with what we're talking about here. Guys are all the same when it comes to liking a girl. Either they do or they don't. And Josh *does*."

Rebecca sighed. "How do you know?"

"You're asking me?" Kathy exclaimed. "You should know! You're the one he kissed!"

"But that's just it," said Rebecca in frustration. "Josh isn't like me, he's not inexperienced and shy. He's probably kissed a hundred girls, including Monica DeForest." She gulped to keep her tears back. "Kissing me didn't have to mean anything to him."

"That's not what you seemed to think when you came in last night," Kathy said, gently reminding her.

"Oh, I don't know. I did feel close to him. But then it was like it all turned around on me. I'm not cool enough. I'm not *together* enough." Rebecca flopped back on the bed and stared glumly at the ceiling.

Kathy studied her friend for a moment and then clasped her hands together decisively. "Well," she said in a practical tone, "I can see that what you need is something to boost your confidence. And since *words* haven't done it, let's take some *action*!" She jumped up and looked down at Rebecca critically. "What are you going to wear this afternoon?"

"To the *beaver* pond?" Rebecca looked blank. "I suppose I'll wear what I've got on."

"Wrong," said Kathy in a determined voice. "You can't wear ordinary clothes unless you want to feel ordinary." She opened Rebecca's drawers and furiously began going through her things. Rebecca got off her bed and stood behind her, watching.

"I could wear my Laura Ashley jumper," she said. "That's pretty."

"Wrong again," said Kathy. "Pretty is not what we're after. You need something relaxed, free, wild— I've got it!" She abandoned Rebecca's drawers and pulled open one of her own. "I know I brought them—"

Rebecca looked over Kathy's shoulder as her friend slammed that drawer shut and yanked open another one.

"Here they are!" Kathy announced. From underneath a pile of underwear she proudly pulled out a pair of hot pink stirrup pants.

"You want me to wear *those*?" Rebecca asked in disbelief.

"Why not?" asked Kathy. "I brought them for a special occasion, and this is it!"

Rebecca slowly took the pants from Kathy and examined them. "Kathy, these pants are— well, they're not *me*."

"But you always said you loved them," Kathy said, acting hurt.

"I do love them," Rebecca said. "I love them on *you*. But I don't know if I could really wear them myself. Besides, pink isn't a good color for me and they'd be too long." She handed the pants back to Kathy.

"Just try them on! They're stretch pants, so they should be okay." Kathy pushed the pants back at Rebecca.

Rebecca hesitated.

"Please, Becky, just try them," Kathy said persuasively. "Take it from me, clothes are very important. I should know, I have a ton of them. Different clothes can make you feel like a different person! Isn't that what you want?"

"I guess so." Rebecca held the pants in front of her and looked at her reflection in the mirror. "Okay," she said. "I'll give them a try."

Kathy also produced a lacy tank top and an oversize white cotton sweater with a deep V-neck. After Rebecca put on the whole outfit, Kathy stepped back to survey her.

"How do I look?" Rebecca asked timidly.

"Well, look at yourself in the mirror!" said Kathy. "I think you look great."

What she saw in the mirror made Rebecca want to laugh, but at the same time she was fascinated by the transformation. The clothes actually did fit her, and she looked so *different*. Her heart gave an excited jump.

"What do you think?" Kathy asked with a smile.

"I think I look pretty good," Rebecca said slowly, not really wanting to admit it. "I feel—wild!"

"That's just what we want," Kathy remarked, shaking her finger at Rebecca's face like a schoolteacher. "A wild girl is never shy! Now for some makeup. It's a must with your new look."

Rebecca let Kathy apply the cosmetics and then looked at herself again. She gasped.

"Wow," she said quietly. "Now I really do look different."

"You look like a model," Kathy said, pleased. "And as we both know, that's the kind of girl Josh likes."

Rebecca was still worried. "But that doesn't solve all my problems. What if I get tongue-tied?"

"Just talk!" Kathy said. "Use your willpower and force the words out. You can do it. I've seen you."

"But sometimes I just don't know what to talk *about*," said Rebecca.

"Becky, you're smart." Kathy was encouraging. "You can think of something to say if you really try. And don't forget—boys like you to talk about them. Tell Josh how great he is. He certainly won't be bored by that."

Rebecca nodded slowly. She looked at herself in the mirror again and then turned to Kathy and smiled. "Thanks," she said.

"Don't mention it. That's what friends are for."

Rebecca was less nervous now that she had talked to Kathy. With the pink pants on, she felt armed and ready for anything. She glimpsed Josh coming down the path toward the cabin with a knapsack over his shoulder. When he saw Rebecca in the window, he grinned and waved.

"Hi!" she said brightly as Kathy pushed her out onto the porch.

Josh's face fell a little. "Hi," he said back, almost as brightly. Rebecca could tell he was looking at her pants. She felt herself about to blush and clam up, but then remembered Kathy's advice: "Force the words out!"

"Aren't these great?" she said quickly. "I think they're wild."

"They're wild all right," Josh said, shaking his head. He grabbed her hand. "Come on. Let's go!"

They walked past the bathhouses, and then past the clearing by the lake where the barbecue had been the night before. Josh turned down a trail blazed with blue paint on the tree trunks.

He let go of her hand as soon as they had walked a few yards. *He was only being friendly,* Rebecca thought as she tramped along beside him. *I'd better not let up on Kathy's tactics.*

Rebecca took a deep breath and started talking. She gabbed for the entire walk, not even pausing when she and Josh had to hurdle a tree that had fallen across the path. She talked about rock music, mentioning the bands she knew Josh liked, and about how she was going to take up rock guitar instead of classical, because it was "so much cooler." She reminisced about the Hudson Falls High baseball team's season, recapping all Josh's great plays.

Rebecca had never been a chatterbox before and it was a funny sensation to her. It was exhilarating, but at the same time it made her feel like a stranger to herself. And deep inside she had a funny intuition that all her talking was spoiling what could have been a magical walk with Josh.

The path cut back in toward the lake and Josh stopped. "There it is," he said, pointing to what looked like a mound of sticks just off the shore.

Rebecca could hardly focus on the view because she was so light-headed from all her talking. She became silent, and Josh took advantage of the momentary calm to clasp her hand and lead her to the side of the lake. Rebecca sat down awkwardly on the pine needles because she was trying not to get Kathy's pants dirty. Once she was settled she turned hesitantly toward Josh. He was turning toward her at the same time and they both jumped a little.

Rebecca started chattering again. "It's so quiet here," she said loudly. "I love it when it's quiet. I mean, I usually do." She stopped in confusion.

Josh stood up and picked up a stone and skipped it over the lake. "Rebecca, is anything wrong?" he asked casually.

Rebecca's voice went up an octave. "Wrong? Of course not! Things couldn't be better. You know, Josh, I'm not surprised you brought me here." She self-consciously adjusted the revealing neckline of the sweater she was wearing.

"Really?" Josh sounded surprised.

"Well, you know so much about everything," Rebecca explained. "I'm not surprised you know about beaver dams, too."

Josh looked embarrassed. He picked up another stone and skipped it. "I do? I mean, you're not?"

Remembering Kathy's advice, Rebecca caught her breath and rambled on. "You know about sports," she said. "And you're a good student, and you're popular—"

Josh shook his head, puzzled. "Rebecca—" he said.

She didn't miss a beat even though she sensed that Josh wasn't responding the way Kathy had predicted. "I'm sure you'll be elected most popular in the school yearbook next year—"

Josh walked over to the shore, dusting pine needles off his jeans as he went. "If we're quiet," he said, standing with his back to her, "maybe we'll see a beaver."

Rebecca fought back a sudden feeling of loss and disappointment. *I blew it,* she thought sadly. *I blew it worse than if I hadn't tried not to blow it.* She buried her face in the soft fabric of the stirrup pants on her pulled-up knees and then sat up again. *I hate these pants!* she wanted to shout.

Rebecca's silence seemed to have given Josh a chance to get his thoughts together, and now he turned and strolled back to where she was sitting. He squatted next to her and looked into her face, his blond eyebrows wrinkled in concern. Rebecca looked back at him with wide eyes, trying very hard to keep her chin from trembling and her eyes from filling with tears.

"You seem—different today," he said haltingly.

"I think it's nice to be different sometimes," Rebecca said, defending herself. "You know, clothes can make people feel different. I like to experiment."

Rebecca's words sounded hollow even to herself. She knew it wasn't Rebecca Thompson speaking, and she saw from the surprised and disappointed expression in Josh's eyes that he knew it, too. Rebecca knew it wasn't even Kathy McBride talking, even though it was Kathy she was echoing. Coming from Kathy these words would be genuine.

"Rebecca," Josh said, beginning in a tentative voice, "if it's about last night . . ."

Suddenly Rebecca knew that she couldn't let Josh see how much the night before had meant to her. He obviously thought she was a fool—he was going to say it all had been a mistake. She cut him short. "Oh, last night," she said. She tried to sound breezy, but her voice cracked. "Yeah, I'm sorry about that." She waved a hand dismissively, hoping Josh didn't see it shaking.

He seemed taken aback. His eyes narrowed and clouded over. "Yeah, I'm sorry, too." His voice had a hard edge to it. "I hope you didn't think—"

"Oh, no," Rebecca said, too hastily. "Of course not."

Josh stood up abruptly and so did Rebecca. She tried to read his face but it was like a mask.

"Maybe we'd better just go," he said, turning back toward the trail. This time he didn't take her hand. He didn't even look at her. Rebecca was miserable.

They walked back in complete silence. It was certainly a contrast to the trip over, but Rebecca wasn't sure which was worse—her terrible, unnatural chattering or this painful, tense wordlessness.

Josh left her at the cabin with a curt "See you" and a halfhearted wave. Rebecca climbed the steps with legs as heavy as lead, the hot pink stirrup pants weighing her down.

When she walked through the door Kathy, who had been lying on her bed with a magazine, bounced up eagerly. "How was it?" she asked in a chipper voice.

"Awful," Rebecca said dully. "I blew it."

Kathy's face fell. "But you looked great."

"Yeah, I would've looked great if I was going to a 'dress as your best friend' costume party," said Rebecca.

"Well, were you interesting at least?" Kathy asked hopefully.

"No, I wasn't." Rebecca threw herself face down on her bed. "I can't talk now, Kathy. Go to lunch without me. Please." Rebecca heard Kathy leave the cabin on tiptoe. When the door clicked shut, Rebecca started to cry as if she would never stop.

Chapter Eight

Rebecca slept late the next day. She woke up feeling as if her head were stuffed with cotton. Kathy was nowhere in sight, and her empty bed had already been neatly made. Rebecca sat up and peeked out the window. From the height of the sun peeking through the hazy clouds she guessed it might be past breakfast time.

Rebecca climbed out of bed and started to dress. After pulling on a clean pair of jeans and a white shirt, she sat on the edge of the bed and reached for her boots. As she did so she caught sight of her sneakers, which where spattered with mud from her walk with Josh. She bit her lip to stop tears from springing to her eyes. *I'm not going to think about it,* she thought grimly. *I'll just forget it ever happened.* One tear managed to squeeze out and trickle down her cheek. *I'll never really forget*, she thought. *But I can try.*

Rebecca started for the cook house, hoping she'd be able to get something. She might be brokenhearted but that didn't keep her from being hungry. And maybe Kathy would still be around—she'd be happy for the company.

As she passed her parents' cabin she saw the door was ajar. She climbed up the stairs and looked in.

Her mother was sitting in a rocking chair with Melissa braced between her knees, struggling to fix the zipper on her younger daughter's yellow windbreaker. She gave Rebecca a bright smile. "Hi, honey!" She pulled the zipper up with a jerk. "There we are, Melissa."

Melissa skipped past Rebecca onto the porch. "I'm going fishing!" she announced cheerfully. "First I have to dig worms, though. Okay, Mommy?"

"Okay, Mel," Mrs. Thompson called after her.

Rebecca grinned. "She's having a good time."

Mrs. Thompson gave Rebecca a hug. "And how about you?"

"Sure, Mom," Rebecca said, turning toward the door. She didn't trust herself not to start bawling in front of her mother. "I haven't eaten yet. I just stopped by on my way to the cook house."

Mrs. Thompson followed Rebecca outside, shutting the cabin door behind her. "I know," she said. "Your dad and I looked in on you this morning and you were dead to the world. He wanted to say goodbye before he took off for Calgary. He has an evening session today so he's staying overnight."

Mrs. Thompson beckoned to Melissa, and the three started down the wooded path to the cook house. Rebecca thought about how she and Josh had walked there together on the first day. She was amazed that she had managed to ruin everything in such a short time.

"Josh asked about you at breakfast," Mrs. Thompson said casually, as if reading her daughter's mind.

"That's nice." Rebecca pretended to be absorbed in helping Melissa choose between two potential worm-digging sticks.

"Kathy told us that you weren't feeling well," Mrs. Thompson said.

Rebecca felt a warm rush of gratitude for Kathy's quick thinking. "I'm not sick or anything," she told her mother. "I was just super tired for some reason."

Mrs. Thompson nodded sympathetically. She put an arm lightly around Rebecca's shoulders, and the two walked along in companionable silence for a few minutes while Melissa trotted ahead of them.

"You know, I remember being your age, Becky," her mother said suddenly. "Sixteen is fun, but it can also be hard."

Rebecca smiled to herself. She should have known her mom would see right through her and know that something was wrong.

"I liked a boy when I was sixteen." Mrs. Thompson laughed. "Just being with him was the most important thing in the world to me. I was hopelessly distracted!"

"Was it Dad?" Rebecca asked curiously.

"Oh, no," Mrs. Thompson said with another laugh. "I met your father much later. That's an entirely different story!" She dropped her arm so she and Rebecca could kneel by Melissa, who was investigating the mud at the bank of the stream for worms. "That's nice, Mel," Mrs. Thompson said as Melissa proudly displayed one.

"Yuck!" exclaimed Rebecca.

They had neared the Valoises' house where Mrs. Thompson and Melissa planned to stop. Mrs. Thompson turned to Rebecca again. "What I'm trying to say, sweetie, is that if you want to talk about anything—about Josh maybe—I'd be happy to listen."

Rebecca smiled. "Thanks, Mom, but unfortunately there's not much to talk about where Josh is concerned. If you know what I mean."

"Well, the offer still stands." Mrs. Thompson took one of Melissa's small hands after making sure it didn't contain a worm. "We're off to fish. Have a nice morning, hon!"

Rebecca trudged the rest of the way to the cook house. Her talk with her mother had made her feel better and worse at the same time. It was nice to know someone else had been through what she was going through and lived to tell about it. But she didn't want to hear that her mother had loved a boy when she was sixteen and then forgotten all about him. That thought was far too depressing.

On her way in the door, she almost bumped into Clyde. She took a look at the deserted tables and then asked him, "Have you seen Kathy, Clyde?"

Clyde pointed to the big house. "I think she's at the house. Glad to see you're getting some breakfast, Becky." He nodded approvingly. "Riding horses takes a lot of energy."

Rebecca grabbed some orange juice and a blueberry muffin. She sat down just long enough to gulp the juice and swallow the muffin and then she headed out again.

The field between the cook house and the Valoises' house was a profusion of color. Wild roses and daisies sprang from the grass, smelling even prettier than they looked. Ordinarily Rebecca would have stopped to enjoy the sights and scents, but that day her mood was so solidly gray there wasn't any room for color.

When she got nearer to the house, she spotted her mother and Mrs. Valois on the porch.

"Morning, Mrs. Valois! Hi, Mom," Rebecca called out. "Has either of you seen Kathy?"

Mrs. Valois pointed in the direction of the backyard. "They're playing horseshoes," she said.

"Thanks!" Rebecca waved.

As she walked around the side of the house, she heard Kathy laughing. The blueberry muffin in Rebecca's stomach started to feel like a brick as she realized that Kathy wasn't alone.

Kathy and Josh were standing, deep in conversation, with their backs to Rebecca. Kathy was giggling at something Josh had said. She was leaning close to him in an intimate way. They were both holding horseshoes, but it looked to Rebecca as if they had forgotten all about the game. *Or they're playing a new one*, she thought, too hurt to feel angry. She looked around for Eric, hoping that he was somewhere near, that Kathy and Josh's togetherness wasn't what it appeared. But her brother was nowhere in sight.

Rebecca took one last look around the side of the house. Kathy had put a hand on Josh's shoulder and now they seemed to be talking seriously. Rebecca didn't need to see anymore. She started to run, not stopping until she reached the barn. She ducked into the empty stall next to Gingernut's and collapsed in the hay, hot tears pouring down her face.

How can Kathy do this to me? Rebecca thought forlornly. *Sure she's famous for flitting from boy to boy, but I thought she liked Eric. Forget Eric!* Rebecca wiped at a new flood of angry tears. *I thought she liked me! I thought she was my best friend.*

Suddenly Rebecca felt more sad and alone than she ever had in her life. It was Kathy she had always turned to when things got her down, and now Kathy was betraying her. She sniffled. *Okay, I've got to get ahold of myself,* she decided. *Maybe I'm not being fair to Kathy. After all, she gave me every chance to get together with Josh. She really tried to help me. It's not her fault I'm such a failure. And Josh has a right to like anyone he wants.*

Rebecca had just caught her breath when she burst into tears all over again. It was no use trying to reason herself out of her jealousy and unhappiness. She had seen what she had seen. Josh liked Kathy, and who could blame him? She was one of the prettiest girls at Hudson Falls High—and Monica DeForest's spitting image. And Kathy didn't have frizzy hair and freckles.

Rebecca heard a footstep at the stall door and looked up, startled with tear-filled eyes. Guy looked back at her, just as startled.

"Oh, Becky!" He sounded embarrassed. "Um,

I was just going to lay some fresh bedding in this stall. Uh—you want to brush Gingernut? Her coat needs some work."

Rebecca jumped to her feet, horrified at being caught crying. Guy didn't make a fuss over her, though. As she passed him he put a curry brush and a blue handkerchief in her hand and smiled at her sympathetically.

"Thanks, Guy," she said, blowing her nose.

"Anytime, Becky."

She went into Gingernut's stall and the chestnut mare snorted a greeting. As she ran the brush along Gingernut's neck, her tears started again. "Oh, Gingernut," she said into the horse's tangled mane. "I wish people were as easy to understand as horses."

Rebecca was late for lunch, and when she got there she wished she hadn't bothered to go at all. Working in the barn had made her feel a little better, but the sight of Eric, Kathy, and Josh happily sitting together brought back the pain and anger even worse than before. All three looked her way as she came in. Eric waved and Kathy threw her a smile. *How dare she smile at me*, Rebecca thought furiously. *What nerve!*

Josh had half stood as if he were coming to meet her, but Rebecca ignored his gaze and went straight to the grill to put in her order. In an instant Kathy was standing next to her.

"How are you?" she whispered.

"Just dandy!" Rebecca snapped.

Kathy looked at her in concern. "Becky, you shouldn't take what happened with you and Josh yesterday so hard."

Rebecca reached for some carrot sticks for Gingernut and stuffed them in her pocket. She didn't bother to respond.

Kathy hesitated and then tried again. "I told everybody you weren't feeling well," she whispered.

"Thanks for all your *help*, Kathy," Rebecca said as cuttingly as she could. She turned away from the grill to leave, but Kathy was standing in her way.

"Excuse me," Rebecca said in an icy voice.

"Well, aren't you going to sit with us?" Kathy asked.

"Ha!" Rebecca laughed scornfully.

Kathy looked more confused than ever, but she refused to budge. "Are you at least going to tell me what's bugging you?" Rebecca remained silent. Kathy threw her hands up, clearly irritated. "Well, suit yourself, Becky. If you want to sulk, go ahead."

Kathy stepped aside and Rebecca sailed by her with her tray. She swerved by the table where Eric and Josh were sitting with their mouths open and sat at one in the farthest corner with her back purposefully to the others.

At first she was still too mad at Kathy to feel upset, but by the time she started on the second half of her hamburger, Rebecca was cooling down and her tears were dangerously near the surface again. She felt left out as she listened for the sound of Josh, Eric, and Kathy's voices. She dropped her napkin on the floor so she could glance at the other table as she picked it up. Kathy was sitting next to Eric facing in Rebecca's direction, but when she saw Rebecca peering at her she stood up abruptly and flounced to the other side of the table by Josh, her back to Rebecca.

Humph! Rebecca said to herself as she bit into a crunchy dill pickle. *So she's decided to flaunt her conquest of Josh. I suppose the next time I look she'll be kissing him in public!* She tried to get her anger back, but sadness was winning out. She looked down at the rest of her hamburger with distaste. There was no point in lingering at lunch under those circumstances.

Rebecca took a deep breath and stood up. She walked by Josh, Eric, and Kathy without a word. Kathy looked up at Rebecca as she passed and saw a tear trailing down Rebecca's flushed cheek.

"Excuse me, you guys," Kathy said. "I'll catch up with you later."

Rebecca had started to run as soon as she

had gotten outside, so Kathy also broke into a trot. At one point Rebecca heard her friend following her and looked over her shoulder. Kathy made such a funny, touching sight flopping along awkwardly in her dressy thong sandals and snug miniskirt that Rebecca wanted to laugh. She reminded herself that Kathy was her enemy now. She would never be able to think a kind thought about her again.

When she got to the cabin, Rebecca flew up the steps and inside, banging the door behind her. She belly flopped onto the bed and tried to catch her breath. It looked like a confrontation was inevitable.

The door burst open and Kathy appeared, panting and windblown. She had taken off her sandals and was waving one of them at Rebecca.

"Do you mind telling me what your problem is, Rebecca Thompson?" she gasped. "Do you mind telling me why you're taking out your disappointment about Josh on me?"

"As if you didn't know!" Rebecca exclaimed. "Benedict."

"Benedict?" Kathy echoed blankly.

"Benedict *Arnold*."

"Benedict Arnold?" Kathy's forehead was wrinkled. "Wait a minute, Becky. Just what do you mean by that?"

"Come off it, Kathy. You know exactly what

I mean. I saw you 'playing horseshoes' with Josh. Don't act so innocent." Rebecca tried to keep her voice even, without complete success.

Kathy let go of her sandals and they clattered to the wood floor. She looked at her friend in amazement. "So you saw me playing horseshoes with Josh. So what?"

"So *what*?" Rebecca shook her head. "How blind do you think I am, Kathy? I know what you were up to!"

Kathy slowly sank down on her own bed. "No, I don't think you do."

"I saw you and Josh," Rebecca said insistently. "And I didn't need my contact lenses to see what was going on between you." She faltered as a sob caught in her throat. "How could you, Kathy?"

Rebecca buried her face in her pillow. Kathy stared over at her. "You know, Becky, you *are* blind, even *with* your lenses!" Rebecca said something that was muffled by the pillow.

Kathy was more hurt than angry. "Becky, are you going to listen to me if I tell you what really happened this morning?" she asked quietly.

Rebecca nodded, her face still hidden.

"Good." Kathy clapped her hands briskly on her knees. "First of all, let me tell you that sometimes it's hard to be your friend."

Rebecca sat up and wiped her eyes, still keeping her expression as cold as possible.

"To make a long story short," Kathy said, "when Josh and I finished eating breakfast at the same time, I suggested stopping by the Valoises'. In all honesty I was looking for an opportunity to be alone with Josh." She saw Rebecca's face begin to crumble and held up her hand. "But not for what you think! I wanted to find out what had happened between you two, and since *you* wouldn't tell me I didn't have much of a choice!"

Kathy paused to catch her breath. Rebecca remained silent except for an occasional sniffle. "Well," Kathy said finally, "don't you have anything to say?"

Rebecca's eyes were glued to the floor and her voice was small. "That's really what you were doing, Kathy?"

"That's it," Kathy said. Her voice had taken on a hard, hurt edge. "I know it's tough to believe, considering I'm your best friend, but I guess you found it easier to suspect me than have faith in me. I guess we have different definitions of what best friends are, because I would never suspect you of pulling a stunt like that on me."

A tear trickled down Rebecca's already tear-stained face. "I'm sorry. I do have faith in you. I always have. You're the best friend in

the world. I don't know what came over me."
Kathy bounced to her feet and onto Rebecca's
bed to throw her arms around her and give
her a squeeze.

"I'll forgive you if you've forgiven me!" she
exclaimed. "Even though I didn't do anything
wrong in the first place."

"Of course I forgive you!" Rebecca returned
her friend's hug with all her might. "I don't
have any excuse for jumping to conclusions
so unfairly." She pushed a rebellious strand
of hair out of her eyes. "Except, well, sometimes it's hard to be *your* friend."

Kathy looked surprised. "What do you mean?
I thought I was the easiest person in the
world to get along with!" she said teasingly.

"You are," Rebecca said. "But I can't help
comparing myself to you sometimes. In most
ways you're everything I'm not but wish I
were. You're pretty and popular and outgoing
and talkative and stylish—"

"Stop!" Kathy said, interrupting. "There you
go again! Don't sell yourself short. You're not
me, but so what? You're *you* and that's special enough. Which leads me to my second
confession of the day. Are you ready?"

Rebecca frowned, puzzled. "Shoot!"

"Well"—Kathy took a deep breath and rolled
her eyes ruefully—"this is hard for me to say,
but—I made a big mistake!"

Rebecca laughed.

Kathy continued, "Unbelievable, right? But I did. Becky, I made a mistake getting you all dressed up for your date with Josh and telling you to talk up a storm on all his favorite subjects."

"But it works for you," Rebecca said. "It's not your fault I couldn't pull it off."

"That's just it," said Kathy. "That's my style, not yours. And as Josh hinted to me, your style has been working just fine."

Rebecca turned to her friend with eager eyes. "*What* did Josh hint at?"

"Well, as I was *going* to tell you as soon as I got a chance . . ." Kathy paused teasingly. Rebecca gave an impatient bounce. "He likes *you*! He likes *your* style."

"Did he say that?" Rebecca couldn't believe it.

"Not in so many words," Kathy said. "Josh is pretty reserved and I was trying not to be too nosy. But believe me, it wasn't that hard to figure out."

Rebecca's whole world had turned back around. If her friend was right, then she hadn't blown it with Josh.

"What do I do now?" she asked.

Kathy thought for a moment, her head tilted to one side, blond hair swinging. "Now? Now you just relax and let things happen naturally. I don't dress you up, you don't pretend to be something you're not. And day after tomorrow, we're going on an overnight camp-out—talk about the perfect setting for romance!" Kathy giggled and Rebecca was surprised to see her blush a little. "Actually, I'm counting on it to bring out the romance in Eric, too!"

"Really?" Rebecca wrinkled her nose and laughed. "I was going to say, 'I don't know what you see in him,' but I guess I'm not a fair judge." She winked. "Aw, I guess he's not so bad, even if he is my brother!"

Chapter Nine

The next day passed uneventfully for Rebecca. She only saw Josh in passing—he was off fishing and hiking with Eric, while she and Kathy swam and rode and visited with Mrs. Valois.

That night Rebecca baby-sat for Melissa at her parents' cabin while Mr. and Mrs. Thompson went into Calgary to the theater. Kathy had gone to the boys' cabin to play some cards, although she claimed she wouldn't stay long because she was tired and wanted to rest up for their big day.

Rebecca was very excited about the overnight pack ride. When she had met Josh to say "hi" that day, she thought she had detected some encouraging warmth there. If only she had heard the things Kathy told her from Josh, then she'd be completely confident. All she could do was wait and see. And if Kathy were wrong, well, Rebecca could learn to live with that. She might not end up with Josh, but she was ending up with a better understanding of herself. She would learn to live without Josh's liking her.

Mr. and Mrs. Thompson were home by midnight and found their elder daughter nodding over her book. They packed her off to her own cabin.

Rebecca stumbled down the dimly lit path, still half-asleep. She was yawning so hard as she approached her cabin that she didn't notice the two embracing figures until she was practically on top of them.

Kathy and Eric broke apart, embarrassed. "Uh, hi, Becky!" Kathy said brightly. Eric looked sheepish.

"Hi, guys!' Rebecca pointed to the cabin, picking up her pace as she walked by them. "I'm going—in there—to bed. Good-night!" She sprinted up the stairs, stifling a giggle. The thought of Kathy and Eric liking each other still struck Rebecca as funny, but also kind of nice. She put on her pajamas and crawled into bed in the dark.

From outside Rebecca heard the sound of low voices and laughter. She lay on her side, her face toward the window, through which a ray of moonlight streamed. Rebecca sighed. She squeezed her eyes tightly shut. It could still happen for her and Josh. Her vacation in the Canadian Rockies wasn't over yet!

The next morning was clear and sunny. Rebecca, Eric, Kathy, and Josh sat mounted at the corral gate, their bedrolls strapped to their saddles, their horses nickering eagerly. Clyde and Guy were busy securing provisions on the two packhorses.

Josh, Eric, and Kathy looked a lot more comfortable on horseback than they had just a few days before, and the whole group was in high spirits, Rebecca not least of all. She joined in the joking and laughing, determined not to worry about what her brother and Josh might have thought of her scene in the dining hall the other day.

The only new development in their group dynamics was that Kathy and Eric were more openly attentive to each other. Eric maneuvered Clown next to Mac so he could tease her about her very un-Kathy-like riding outfit of jeans and a sweatshirt. When their horses nuzzled each other, Eric leaned over and gave Kathy a quick kiss on the cheek. "The horses've got the right idea," he said.

Josh had moved Joan of Arc nearer Rebecca and Gingernut and now he grinned sheepishly. "I don't know about those two," he said with a smile to Rebecca. "Could be a deadly combination!"

Rebecca laughed. "I agree completely. I don't trust Eric with my best friend, and I don't trust Kathy with my brother!"

"It looks like they're going to need some chaperoning on this trip. We'd better make sure they don't do anything we wouldn't do."

Josh's eyes were friendly as he looked down at her, and Rebecca warmed to his glance in a way she never had before. She still felt a little timid, but somehow it was easier now to smile back. They hadn't talked alone since their disastrous date, and while there was definitely a feeling of something unresolved between them, it wasn't a bad feeling. And Josh's last comment made her tingle right down to her toes.

A few hours out from the Kicking Horse, Clyde suggested they take a rest. The steepest part of the trail was just ahead. The sun was high in the sky by this time and the spot they chose to picnic in, a grassy meadow looking out over the canyon, was sun warmed and dry. They tethered their horses and sprawled on the grass, digging into their lunches.

When the four guys began a second round of sandwiches, Kathy and Rebecca moved off to one side. After spreading out their sweatshirts, they lay with their faces to the sun. Kathy let out a deep, satisfied sigh. "This is what I really need right now," she said. "A nap!"

"You had a late night, huh?" Rebecca said.

"Don't you know it!" Kathy giggled. "Do you think I'm a total creep now because I'm falling in love with your twin brother?"

Rebecca snorted. "I've always known you were weird. So it's nothing new!"

The two girls giggled helplessly. They only laughed harder when Eric and Josh strolled over to ask what was so funny. Eric was about to start tickling Kathy to make her share the joke, when Clyde and Guy motioned to them.

"Let's mount up, everybody!" Guy said. "The horses are tired of waiting." When they were all in the saddle, he said, "Take it easy on this last part of the trail. Trust your horses— they're used to the trip."

The last hour of the trail was extremely difficult. The path got narrower and curved much more often. But Rebecca felt completely safe. Gingernut picked her way delicately along the rocky path and Rebecca held the reins lightly, leaning into the mare's movement.

At every switchback, Rebecca caught glimpses of the mountains adjacent to their destination, a giant meadow called Cornflower Blue, and the tops of the trees in the green valley below. The snowcapped peaks of even higher mountains across the valley made the panorama even more dramatic. Rebecca wished her parents could have seen the vistas, but understood that they hadn't wanted to leave Melissa behind. And, anyway, the sleep-over wouldn't have been quite so much fun with them along!

Just above the tree line, the trail narrowed to a little path bordered on one side by big round boulders and flat-topped rock formations. Words carved into one of the rocks announced their arrival at Cornflower Blue. They rounded the last corner and the trail suddenly opened onto a glorious meadow filled with purple blue heather.

"Wahoo! We're here!" Eric hollered, flipping his cowboy hat in the air.

They all dismounted and began to inspect the campsite. Some rocks were arranged in a circle around a cleared-out space, ready-made for a fire. Clyde pointed to some larger bare patches. "That's where we'll set up our tents. Let's unload!"

Kathy fumbled with the buckles of her saddlebag. Like Rebecca, she couldn't take her eyes from the flowers in the field. "Why is it called Cornflower Blue?" she asked as she swung her bedroll free. "All I see is purple!"

Clyde chuckled. "In a certain light, just before sunset, the field looks more blue. Maybe the person who first laid eyes on it saw it at just that moment."

Kathy's eyes grew dreamy. "How romantic!" she said.

Eric was more practical. "How are we going to make a fire tonight?" he wondered. "There aren't any trees around for wood."

Clyde pointed a few yards from the campsite. Eric saw a good-sized stack of wood hidden in the high grass.

"Where'd that come from?" he asked.

"The management," said Clyde with a wink. "At Kicking Horse Ranch we try to make sure our guests are comfortable, no matter where we take them!"

Rebecca had spied an outcropping of rocks at the edge of the meadow, beyond which seemed to be nothing but clouds. "What's out there?"

"The nicest lookout point you've ever seen," said Guy. "It goes one hundred and eighty degrees."

Josh had come up behind them. "Let's check it out!" he suggested to Rebecca. He grabbed her hand and Eric grabbed Kathy's, and the four of them waded out into the high purple heather. Rebecca's heart pounded at Josh's touch. She liked the way it felt to run with him through the meadow.

For a moment they all shared a relaxed, happy silence, sitting on the sun-baked rocks. Circling them were mountaintops, each with its own distinctive shape.

"That one looks like an Indian head," Josh said, pointing to a jagged peak.

"That one looks like a giant loaf of bread," said Kathy, pointing to another one.

"I see a penguin," Eric said.

"What do *you* see, Becky?" Kathy asked.

Rebecca gazed across the mountain range, pretending to study each peak seriously. "There! A hot fudge sundae with a cherry on top!" Only afterward, when the others had stopped laughing, did Rebecca realize that she had forgotten to be tongue-tied and shy.

"Come on down, gang!" Guy called from the campsite. "We still have to put up the tents. The sun will be setting before you know it."

Rebecca, Eric, and Kathy had never been camping before, so they needed lessons from the other three on setting up tents. Guy and Eric worked on the tent the two ranch hands would occupy while Clyde and Kathy set up the girls' quarters and Rebecca and Josh the boys'.

As Josh showed her how to set in the small stakes that anchored the tent ropes Rebecca found herself holding her breath. She wanted him to say something to her—anything, as long as it was vaguely personal.

After they had finished with the tent and were inspecting it, Josh turned to Rebecca and looked as if he might be about to make some sort of confession. "Rebecca," he said, his voice low.

"Yes?" she responded, wide-eyed.

Just then Eric yelled in their direction. "Come take a look at Camp Fire Girl Kathy's masterpiece!"

Josh and Rebecca stepped apart from each other, suddenly shy. Rebecca walked quickly back toward the others, pretending to be eager to look at the tent she'd be sleeping in.

Kathy displayed it proudly. "I really checked the ground carefully for bumps, Becky," she said. "I even swept it with a little broom made of heather! We'll both have a level spot to put our sleeping bags on."

"Well, I'm impressed," Rebecca admitted. "I've never seen you do housework in your life!"

Kathy grinned. "I know—it's never been my thing. But this was fun—no vacuum cleaner involved!"

The two girls spent a few minutes unpacking the few things they had brought with them.

"No place to plug in my hair dryer," Kathy said. "But other than that . . ."

When they emerged from the tent they caught a whiff of smoke. Clyde had started a campfire. Rebecca suddenly realized she was hungry and looked at her watch. It was almost dinnertime. The day had flown by. When she and Kathy joined Clyde they saw that he'd opened the cooler. There were hamburgers and hot dogs, potato salad, and fixings for s'mores. Rebecca's mouth watered.

The girls helped Clyde with the meal while Guy, Josh, and Eric took the horses to a stream nearby for water. Soon they were all sitting around the fire with tin plates piled high.

Eric spoke up first, in between hot dogs. "Hey! It's just about sunset. We should go watch it from the lookout."

Clyde looked to the west and his eyes narrowed. "I don't know, folks. It looks like some clouds snuck in when we weren't looking. I think we've seen the last of the sun for the day."

Rebecca followed his gaze, and sure enough, a bank of dark gray clouds had moved in, and with them had come a breeze. With the sun obscured, it was suddenly cool. She shivered.

Josh was sitting next to her, and when he noticed her shiver he moved closer, which only made her shiver again. "Cold?" he asked, his gray eyes looking deeply into her green ones.

"Um—yeah," Rebecca said, her flaming cheeks contradicting her words.

"Here." Josh took off his faded denim jacket and put it around her. His hands lingered on her shoulders, and he held her gaze for a moment longer than was necessary. Finally he shook his head and looked away with a mysterious smile.

Rebecca snuggled into the jacket, breathing in its wonderful scent—denim and Josh. Clyde tossed Josh a bag of marshmallows, and soon they were all toasting them over the fire. Twilight was descending quickly.

"So you see why this place is called Cornflower Blue, eh?" Guy stood up and looked toward the meadow.

Rebecca gasped. Without their even noticing it, a transformation had taken place. In the change of light, everything—rocks, grass, flowers—had taken on a bluish haze.

The sounds of night began to surround them, and Clyde told a ghost story about a woman who had lost her sweetheart one foggy night in the meadow of Cornflower Blue. "She never got over her sorrow," he said, concluding. "And every full moon her ghost appears in the field looking for her lost love."

"I'm glad it's not a full moon tonight!" Eric exclaimed, breaking the spell. "I wouldn't want to run into a ghost up here."

"Me, either," said Kathy vehemently.

"I don't want to scare you folks," said Clyde with a laugh. "But what I see up there is a full moon."

The moon had broken through the clouds above them as he spoke.

The girls giggled nervously. "Like I was

saying," Eric said, "I hope there's a full moon tonight. I'm not afraid of an old lady ghost!"

Just then a flash of lightning lit up the meadow, and only seconds later thunder clapped, the boom echoing long off the granite walls of the surrounding mountains. Kathy squealed and even Clyde and Guy jumped.

"Whoa, where did *that* come from?" Josh exclaimed. He looked down at Rebecca in surprise as she looked up at him with the same expression. When she had jumped at the sound of the thunder, she almost landed in his lap. Quickly, she moved back to her space on the log.

"Looks like we're in for a bit of a storm." Guy's voice was nonchalant, and Rebecca, who was close to panic at the thought of being caught on a mountaintop in a storm in the middle of the night, immediately felt calmer. "Yep." He nodded. "Wind's picked up. Didn't expect this, but what's camping without a little rain so we really know we're sleeping outside?"

Kathy grimaced. "I'm fully conscious of the fact that I'm in the great outdoors! I don't need an extra reminder."

Eric wiped a raindrop from his nose. "Well, here it comes, like it or not!"

The rain didn't begin as a drizzle—right away it was coming down in bucketfuls. Rebecca, Kathy, Josh, and Eric ran shrieking and laughing for the nearest tent, while Guy yelled that he and Clyde were going to retether the horses at the far end of the meadow.

The four campers squeezed inside the girls' tent on their hands and knees and collapsed in a wet, giggling pile. After a moment they caught their breath, untangled themselves, and sat up. Josh and Eric had to hunch over because the tent was so low.

"Not exactly built for a double date, huh?" said Eric with a mischievous grin.

There was another flash of lightning, and that time the thunder came almost simultaneously. Kathy just about leapt into Eric's arms. "Do you think our tent could get struck by lightning?" she asked nervously.

"Not a chance," Eric assured her. "Not while I'm in charge!"

"Gee, that's comforting," Rebecca said.

"It sounds like the rain's coming down harder than before," said Josh. "You girls have houseguests for a while at least. How're you going to entertain us?"

"Let's play a game!" Rebecca said.

"How about truth-or-dare?" Kathy said.

"Okay," Eric said. "But only if Becky promises not to tell mom and dad."

Rebecca crossed her heart. "On my honor," she said solemnly.

"So—who wants to start?" Kathy looked at

each of them in turn, her blue eyes sly and laughing.

Rebecca was suddenly very conscious of how close they were all sitting in the tent. She could feel the warmth of Josh's body next to hers. *Truth-or-dare,* she suddenly thought, agonized. *What if someone asks me a personal question? What if I have to confess to my crush on Josh?* She gulped and crossed her fingers. *Don't pick on me,* she prayed silently.

Kathy's eyes rested on Josh. "Okay, baseball hero," she said playfully. "You shoot first!"

"You asked for it!" He looked from her to Eric. "Who made the first move between you two?"

"Boring question!" Eric waved a hand dismissively, but Kathy laughed.

"No, I'll answer it," she said, running her fingers through her damp hair. "He did, of course. He kissed me, entirely against my will!" She gave Eric a devilish smile.

"What?" he exclaimed. "That's *not* the way it happened at all!" He looked at Josh and Rebecca with wide, innocent eyes. "There I was, the innocent boy-next-door, and she overpowered me with her worldly charms."

Kathy threw a sweatshirt at him. "Cut!" said Rebecca. "Next question!"

Kathy spoke up. "My turn! Now I'm going to get personal with *you,* Josh." She glanced at Rebecca and winked. "I've been wondering about this for a long time. So, Josh—" She paused dramatically. "Who's the pretty girl in the picture in your locker?"

She looked triumphantly at Rebecca, who wanted nothing more at that moment than to disappear. All the charitable thoughts Rebecca had been having about Kathy since their big talk disappeared. Her heart sank as she realized that, in a moment, she might know the absolute worst, what she had been pushing from her mind since they had left on the trip.

Eric hooted. Josh looked surprised, but not dismayed. He nodded his head at Kathy and grinned. "You got me," he said. "I confess. It's a picture of my ex"—Rebecca liked the way he emphasized the syllable—"my *ex*-girlfriend, Monica." Rebecca gasped unintentionally. Josh gave her a questioning look. "Monica Kimball," he said. Rebecca gasped again, this time with relief. "Do you know her?" he asked.

"No, but I wish I did!" Rebecca said sincerely.

"But if she's your *ex*-girlfriend, why do you still have her picture in your locker?" Kathy asked.

Josh laughed sheepishly. "Well, to tell you the truth, I put it there to remind me of something." His tone suddenly became serious. "Something I don't believe anymore. See,

Monica and I didn't end on the best of terms. She really hurt me, and I kept her picture around to remind myself that I didn't want to get involved with anyone in Hudson Falls. But then I met—I changed my mind," he said, finishing awkwardly, a faint flush creeping over his tanned cheeks.

Josh's eyes were on Rebecca, and she wanted to burst out laughing, burst into tears, throw her arms around Kathy, throw her arms around *Josh,* all sorts of crazy things. Instead, she just smiled, shyly but happily.

Kathy and Eric exchanged a glance. "Well," Eric said briskly. "I think I just heard Guy and Clyde calling. I bet they need help with the horses. Come on, Kath! We'll have to risk getting soaked and running into the ghost. See you!"

He grabbed Kathy's hand, and they crawled out of the tent, giggling.

Rebecca and Josh were alone. Rebecca was amazed to find that she wasn't nervous at all. There was more room in the tent then, but Josh continued to sit close to her. There was nothing she wanted more at that moment than for him to kiss her. And she had a feeling she wouldn't have long to wait, but first she had one question to ask.

"So, Josh," she began hesitantly. "You never dated Monica DeForest?"

"Monica DeForest?" Josh shook his head, looking blank. "Why on earth do you ask that?"

"Oh, never mind," Rebecca said cheerfully. She and Josh sat in silence for a few seconds, and then she noticed that the distance between them was growing smaller—from half a foot, to two inches, to no distance at all. They kissed, and Rebecca thought she had never experienced anything so wonderful. She felt relaxed and comfortable and totally *right*, not self-conscious at all. Josh's arms felt warm and reassuring around her, and his lips felt the same.

As they parted he ran a hand through her thick, loose hair.

"I love it when you wear it down," he said softly. "You have the most beautiful hair."

"Me?" Rebecca asked doubtfully. "I'd give anything for it to be straight."

"Nah. It's perfect. It's *you*. And when you let it hang loose it makes you more—you."

He leaned forward and kissed her again. "I've been wanting to do that since the last time we did it," he admitted.

"Even after the beaver dam?" Rebecca shook her head. "I don't know how you can even look at me after I made such a fool of myself!"

"But you didn't," Josh said. He winked. "I understood where you were coming from— after a while! I knew you were just nervous.

And that's okay. I know you're shy—I don't mind."

Rebecca lowered her eyes. "Well, I've always minded," she said quietly. "I've always hated being shy. It's such a curse! I have to tell you," she said, now laughing despite herself, "that I have always been ten times more nervous and shy around you than anyone else. When I think of all the times I made a total fool of myself in front of you, it makes this moment even more unbelievable!"

"Like when?" Josh asked with a perfectly straight face.

"Like when?" Rebecca stared at him, then burst out laughing when he winked.

"Like after the baseball game when you lost your contact lens?" he asked, putting a strong, warm arm around her shoulders.

Rebecca giggled. "Now that's a great example. How could you ever take me seriously after I pulled a stunt like that?"

"I'll admit it took all my self-control not to laugh my head off at the time." Josh's eyes crinkled in a smile. Rebecca looked a little hurt, and he quickly added, "Not because you looked silly—it was just so funny. I thought you were so *cute*." He touched the tip of her nose lightly with his fingertip. Rebecca smiled.

"Did you think I was cute even when I wore

those horrible old glasses?" she asked. "Tell the truth!"

Josh looked solemn. "I thought you were cuter than ever. I loved those glasses! I've been waiting for you to wear them again some-time but you never do. Your new lenses must be harder to lose than your old ones."

"You're terrible!" Rebecca exclaimed.

"I know," said Josh.

As she looked into his eyes and they smiled together, Rebecca thought she must be the happiest person in the world. She had never felt so warm and secure, so comfortable and so—*herself*. It had been a long, rocky road to that moment, but it was worth it.

Josh was watching her closely. "You look serious all of a sudden," he observed. "You look cute when you're serious."

"I was just thinking," said Rebecca, "that I've wanted so much to change these past few months. I wanted to be someone else— Rebecca, not Becky, someone cool and not shy and serious, grown-up instead of cute."

Josh shrugged. "But that's just it, Rebecca. Being called something different doesn't make you a different person. It's all inside—it's how you feel about yourself." He looked in her eyes. "And you should feel great about your-self. You're wonderful," he said sincerely.

"Wonderful?" Rebecca shook her head with

a doubtful smile. "You mean you don't think I'm a nerd because I spend a lot of time in the library and I'm not part of the popular crowd and I play classical guitar instead of rock?"

"Hey, you make all those things sound negative when they're not at all."

"Well, I was just always so scared that you would never like me because we had such different styles."

"No, I was scared!" Josh said. "I thought *you'd* never like *me* because I wasn't in the smart crowd like Len Seaver."

"Len Seaver!" Rebecca groaned. "And I thought you only dated models!"

They both laughed for a solid minute, and when they caught their breath, Josh said, "I guess we wasted a lot of time worrying about things that don't really matter, huh?"

Rebecca heard Eric's and Kathy's voices getting closer, but before they reached the tent, Josh pulled Rebecca to him for one more kiss. That kiss told her more than words ever could. Rebecca wasn't dreaming any longer—her dream had come true.

The next day was sunny and cool. As Rebecca, Josh, Kathy, Eric, Clyde, and Guy rode back to the Kicking Horse Ranch it was as if they were entering a fresh, new rainwashed world. Everything sparkled, and the horses pranced, eager to get home.

Rebecca was tired—she and Kathy had

stayed up most of the night gabbing about Eric and Josh—but it couldn't dim her excitement. Josh was riding behind her on Joan of Arc, and she knew his eyes were on her, and she also knew he was as happy as she was.

As she urged Gingernut into a canter at a level stretch on the trail, she thought of what was in store for her. Two more weeks at the ranch with her family and Kathy and Josh and a whole summer to be in love!

Nothing could be better.

We hope you enjoyed reading this book. If you would like to receive further information about titles available in the Bantam series, just write to the address below, with your name and address:

Kim Prior
Bantam Books
61–63 Uxbridge Road
Ealing
London W5 5SA

If you live in Australia or New Zealand and would like more information about the series, please write to:

Sally Porter
Transworld Publishers (Aust.) Pty. Ltd.
15–23 Helles Avenue
Moorebank
N.S.W. 2170
AUSTRALIA

Kiri Martin
Transworld Publishers (N.Z.) Ltd.
Cnr. Moselle and Waipareira Avenues
Henderson
Auckland
NEW ZEALAND

All Bantam Young Adult books are available at your bookshop or newsagent, or can be ordered from the following address:

Corgi/Bantam Books
Cash Sales Department
PO Box 11
Falmouth
Cornwall
TR10 9EN

Please list the title(s) you would like, and send together with a cheque or postal order. You should allow for the cost of the book(s) plus postage and packing charges as follows:

All orders up to a total of £5.00   50p
All orders in excess of £5.00   Free

Please note that payment must be made in pounds sterling; other currencies are unacceptable.

(The above applies to readers in the UK and Republic of Ireland only)

B.F.P.O. customers, please allow for the cost of the book(s) plus the following for postage and packing: 60p for the first book, 25p for the second book and 15p per copy for the next 7 books, thereafter 9p per book.

Overseas customers, please allow £1.25 for postage and packing for the first book, 75p for the second book, and 28p for each subsequent title ordered.

Thank you!

Janet Quin-Harkin's

Sugar & Spice

Watch out for a smashing new series from the best-selling author, Janet Quin-Harkin.

Meet the most unlikely pair of best friends since Toni and Jill from Janet Quin-Harkin's TEN BOY SUMMER.

Caroline's thrilled to find out she's got a long-lost cousin exactly her age. But she's horrified when Chrissy comes to spend a year with her family. Caroline's a reserved and polite only child – now she has to share her life with a loud, unsophisticated, embarrassing farm girl!

Coming soon – wherever Bantam paperbacks are sold!